Moments in Time...

A Short Story Anthology of Romance

Blue Deco Publishing

www.bluedecopublishing.com

Moments in Time...
A Short Story Anthology of Romance

Cover by Colleen Nye
Editing by Paula Hawkins and Richard Dana Diakun
Formatting by Colleen Nye

Published by Blue Deco Publishing
PO BOX 1663 Royal Oak, MI 48068
BlueDecoPublishing@gmail.com

Copyright © 2017 Blue Deco Publishing & Marianne Wieland
Printed in the United States of America

All rights reserved.

No part of this book may be reproduced or transmitted in any form or by any means, electronic or mechanical, including photocopying, recording or by any information storage and retrieval system, without written permission from the publisher.

The unauthorized reproduction or distribution of a copyrighted work is illegal. Criminal copyright infringement, including infringement without monetary gain, is investigated by the FBI and is punishable by fines and federal imprisonment.

This is a work of fiction. All characters and situations appearing in this work are fictitious. Any resemblance to real persons, living or dead, or personal situations is purely coincidental.

This book is dedicated to Richard and Lisa Diakun with much love and respect for both. Richard's contributions are phenomenal and Lisa's contribution, of which I am sure she was unaware at the time, made for the short story 'The Call'. I thank you both with my whole heart.

Forward

The stories contained in this anthology of romance are a collection of true stories, partially true stories and total fantasy. My imagination can be wild at times and I love to embellish real events to make the content more enjoyable for the readers. However, I do not embellish the actual truth. I also usually leave out the names of the characters to add an air of mystery as to which stories are real and which ones are imagined. There are also some people in the true stories that would rather remain nameless. The stories range from sweet, teenage romance to romance within the elderly population as well as romance of a sort in all the stories in between. Romance is often left up to the interpretation of each individual. After all, what might be romance to one is not necessarily romance to another. So, sit back, get comfortable with a glass of wine, a cup of coffee (yuck), or your favorite beverage and read these stories from my moments in time. See if you can figure out which are real and which are not! Enjoy!

Stories

First Kiss ~ 1

Studio D ~ 7

Too Late... ~ 23

Once in a Lifetime ~ 37

The Call ~ 43

Reconciliation ~ 51

The Scene ~ 59

Come and Get It ~ 65

Finding Rich ~ 79

Friendship & Love Eternal ~ 91

The Reunion ~ 99

The Good Old Days ~ 115

Moments in Time...

First Kiss

She was sitting in the cafeteria with three other girls during lunch period when she saw him for the very first time. She stared at him long enough for the other girls to notice that they no longer held her attention. They began to question her, but as she continued to stare, their voices blended in with the noise in the background. She felt a little dizzy and a slight tingling went from her face all the way down to her toes.

He was beautiful in the classic sense. Easily the cutest boy she had ever seen. He was sitting with two others that she would never remember, and was laughing at something one of the others had said. For a moment, his eyes landed on her and time was frozen in her world. She quickly looked away, her face on fire and her mouth so dry she couldn't speak.

She pretended to listen to the other girls until she was able to look in his direction once again. He was gone. She had waited too long. Her face was hot and she desperately needed some air. The other girls thought she was sick. She thought so, too. She was sure she would not make it through the rest of the day.

They made their way out of the cafeteria, her mind on him, and how in a million years she would never be able to speak to him. She ran into another student and dropped her books forcing her to bend over to retrieve them. She mumbled something about being sorry for not watching where she was going, but was way too embarrassed to make any eye contact.

When she stood up, he was standing there. She couldn't move. He was looking at her and she knew she would burst into flames at any moment. Then she noticed he was holding one of her books and she was so self- conscious, she wanted the floor to open up and swallow her, never to be seen again. But he smiled and she caught the faintest tinge of pink in his cheeks as well.

"You dropped your book," he said.

She took the book, touching his hand as she did so. She noticed he had gone pale and was looking at the wall. That gave her the opportunity to study him a little. God, he was so cute. She felt her heart turn over. He was a little shorter than she was, dark hair, beautiful blue eyes (as it turns out!), and he was dressed nicer than the other boys she came in contact with. She immediately felt that he was the one she wanted. So, she did the only

Moments in Time...

thing she could do. She turned around and bolted into the band room.

It wasn't until later that she noticed he was there too. In the trumpet section. She kept glancing back at him, watching him play. She was sure he was good at it. His lips were perfect and she wanted to 'kiss him senseless.' She had read that recently in some magazines she was too young to be reading. 'True Confessions'. Feelings were coming to the surface that she shouldn't have been having at such a young age. When she thought about it, she was sure he was younger than she was. But she wanted him anyway. She would have to be the aggressor, but she was struggling with self-esteem from some things in her life that had shaped her mind from a very young age. Things even she could not voice.

After a few days of glancing and smiling back and forth, eventually walking in the hall together, and sitting in the same general area at lunch, he took her hand under the table and laced his fingers with hers. She began to tremble deep in her stomach, a feeling she had not had before, but she had read about. She knew then that she wanted to kiss him before the day was over. She hoped he wanted it too.

After school, she met him outside the band room and asked if he could stay and talk to her for a while. He smiled.

"Sure."

Wieland

They went into a deserted classroom, one that she had seen the teacher leave for the day, just minutes ago. They both leaned against the desk, not sure what to do next. He was still holding her hand. More like grasping it from nerves. He was not smiling any longer. His gaze was intense, as was hers. She was trying to look 'smoldering' like the magazine said, but she was sure it wasn't working. She put her hand on his shoulder and he did the same. She could not take her eyes off his lips.

She knew how to kiss. She had learned the year before, but there had been no practice. She leaned in and, thankfully, so did he. Their lips touched for just a brief moment before they both pulled back. He continued to gaze at her and finally went to the door and closed it. There was a radio that he turned on. It was playing a song that (as it turns out) she would not remember, but he would.

He walked back to her and she put her arms around him, as close as she could get. He pulled in closer and kissed her again. She made a decision at that moment to take the kiss to another level. She didn't know how he would take it, but she was going for it anyway. She put her lips on his closed ones and proceeded to open her mouth the way she had done the year before. He responded with enthusiasm. They both pressed in and he very shyly put his tongue in her mouth and she did the same. Maybe he had been reading too.

She came alive with sensation. The trembling started low in her stomach and tingling went all the way

Moments in Time...

from her breasts to her toes. Someone was moaning. She wasn't sure who. She proceeded to follow the magazine and alternated deep kissing him and licking his bottom lip with her tongue. He responded in kind. Then she made another decision and, like the magazine said, she sucked his tongue into her mouth. He was startled at first, but then, he took over as the aggressor, deepening the kisses just as she had done. And he was good. They were good together.

She noticed he was breathing heavy, but she was too. Her heart was pounding and she could feel his against her breast. She wanted him to touch her there, but she wasn't ready to go that far this time. She would need more courage for that and she felt he would as well. The kissing got deeper and he leaned her back over the desk and started kissing her neck. It was definitely her moaning now. She didn't know what to do, so she sat back up and began the kissing all over again. What was probably only minutes seemed like hours. His smell, his lips, she would never forget. She wanted more. Maybe he did too.

They pulled back and looked at each other. Then he smiled and so did she. They took each other's hands and held them close to their hearts.

"Would you like to go to the movies sometime?" He was red in the face as he asked.

"Yes, as long as it is in the back row and we can continue what we started here," she answered.

Wieland

He smiled. "Definitely." And he kissed her again before they left the school together, holding hands and planning other encounters that, as it happened, would shape each of them, for the rest of their lives.

Moments in Time…

Studio D

"Hello? Are you in there?" She was at the door of Studio D in the back hallway of the high school. There was a sign on the door saying 'Do Not Disturb.' She knew that did not mean her. Unless, he was in there with his girlfriend. She tried again.

"Open up or I'm coming in anyway." She hesitated, thinking that maybe he *was* in there with his girlfriend.

"Best friend trumps girlfriend." She didn't want to knock because he said it disturbed his concentration. So, her yelling outside the door didn't? She was tenacious, so she knocked. Loud.

The door opened just a crack and he looked out. "Be quiet! You're loud enough to wake the dead!"

"Well, you're awake now, so let me in." When he hesitated, she gasped, putting both hands over her mouth.

"You aren't alone, are you? You said I was the only one you ever allowed in here. Some best friend you are." She kept firing questions at him. "Did you finally do it? Is that why I can't come in? Is she still in there?" She tried looking around him into the room.

He blocked the way. But he was smiling. He always smiled at her. She was his best friend and she always would be if he had anything to say about it. He could tell her anything, even the fact that he was thinking of 'doing it' soon with his girlfriend. She had a boyfriend too, but he didn't like the guy much. Then, she didn't like his girlfriend much either.

"Okay, you can come in, but no one else. And you can't look at anything I'm writing. It's none of your business." Too late, he realized he had just issued a challenge. She loved a challenge.

"None of my business, huh?" She wrestled with him to see what he was trying to cover. "Music. You're writing a song. Can I hear it? Please, please, please?"

"No! It's not finished. It's for someone very special. I'll make sure you hear it when the time is right." Smooth, he thought. He tried to move the music out of her site, but managed to knock half of his books to the floor instead. Damn, he was clumsy all of a sudden.

Moments in Time...

She bent over to help him pick things up. "You don't have to hide it. I know it's for your girlfriend. I guess all you have to do to get your attention is just flash some boobs outside the window. Head cheerleader or not, your girlfriend lacks class."

"Hey, now," he protested. "No need for you to criticize. She has class."

"Yeah, she does have class," she rebutted. "Six to be exact, and three of those with me. Don't look now, but here she comes, ready to flash you again!"

He tried to cover her eyes and she tried to cover his, before his girlfriend exposed herself. They were laughing and ducking away from each other. He got away just in time to see his girl lift her shirt and squish herself nearly flat against the window. He looked away to see what she thought.

"Oh, gross!" She made a gagging motion with her finger. "What on earth is she doing now? Your wonderful girlfriend is licking the glass."

He quickly turned back to the window to see her swirling her tongue all over the window. *Okay, so that was kind of gross*, he thought to himself. He knew he would be kissing that tongue and playing with those boobs later tonight. He gave her a 'thumbs up' sign and a quick wave before she bounced off back to cheerleading practice. He looked over at his best friend and felt very embarrassed at what she had just witnessed.

"So, your boyfriend is so much better than my girlfriend," he said to cover the red he felt creeping up his face. "He's a moron. He walks around like he's God's gift to women. I have never been able to understand what you see in him."

"He's a trombone player, what can I say? Trombone players are good kissers," she explained as she tried to see the music he'd written. "We've been talking about 'doing it' soon, too. I'm just not sure if it's the right time yet."

"If he's trying to push you into something, I'll kick his ass...if you want."

"You aren't going to kick anybody's ass. You will ruin your 'piano playing' fingers and nobody wants that." She took his hand and put it to her face. "Your hands are amazing, you know."

She changed subjects when she became embarrassed. "Maybe I should have a talk with your girlfriend for displaying what she has, to those of us who are lacking in that area." She glanced down at herself.

He looked at her. "You have nice boobs, too. You shouldn't feel out of place." He put on a funny hat and glasses to make her laugh. He loved to make her laugh.

"What are you talking about? You've never seen my boobs."

Moments in Time...

"I can tell they're nice. Not too big. Not too small." He waved his hands in front of them like he was going to start feeling her up. He dropped his hands, looked her in the eye and winked. "But they're not your best feature."

"Is that right? What do you think is my best feature?" She looked at him somewhere in his nose area, afraid of what he might say.

"Your legs are your best feature. Dancers always have the great legs." He looked down at her legs. "Most of your height is in your legs. You should show them off more. Remember when all four of us went to that concert over in...well, you know the one."

She nodded remembering that he had looked really good that night, too.

"You had on that short skirt and those platform shoes of yours and I about...never mind." He started looking through some stacks of records lying around. She was silent and he wasn't sure that was a good thing. He had to break the silence. "Are we all still going out for pizza after the afternoon's activities?"

"As far as I know." She started looking through the records as well sensing something had changed. And as she did when she felt unsure of herself, she changed the subject again. "Do you want me to help you with your homework?"

"You," he said looking up at her. "You, help me with *my homework?* I have calculus and physics homework. You have drama and more drama." He laughed and pretended to punch her in the arm.

She laughed and punched him back. "We've still got about another hour before our friends are going to be here. What music do you have picked out?"

"Well, I know you really like show tunes, so I picked out some from musicals you've been in. You can sing and dance around if you want."

"That's really sweet." She touched his arm. "I guess we do know a lot about each other. We've been best friends for a long time." She picked out 'Hopelessly Devoted to You', from 'Grease.' "Dance with me," she said.

As the music started, he kissed the back of her hand. "You know I can't dance."

"All you have to do is move, feel the music. You're a musician and you're better than you know. Come here." She stood in front of him and pulled his arms around her, locking her arms over his. They began to just weave back and forth with the music. She began to hum and after a while, to sing along.

He had seen her in many shows in their long friendship. Dancing and singing. He had always been on the outside, but right now he felt he was on the same playing field with her. It felt nice. More than nice. He felt her kiss his cheek. Nothing new. They kissed each other

Moments in Time...

on the cheek all the time. Most kids that didn't know them, thought they were a couple.

The song ended and they broke apart. He put in another song, one he knew was a favorite of hers, 'Summer Lovin'.'

"Hey, we can both sing this one!" She grabbed his hand.

He looked skeptical.

"You know you love me and you would do anything for me," she said.

He took both of her hands as he replied.

"You know I do and I would. I also know you love me too. We've loved each other a long time. Best friends naturally love each other."

She kissed him on the cheek again. "Shut up and sing."

They played around singing the song and acting out the parts and kept grabbing each other around the waist. She stole his hat and put her long hair under it. He pulled the hat off and her hair fell against his face. Her hair had gotten really long. He hadn't noticed until now.

"Let's play a game,' he said. He knew she loved games. "If you had to pick a song for me, what would you pick?"

"That's easy," she said. She picked up a record and put it on the turntable.

He saw what it was. 'You're the One That I Want' and he was a little surprised but covered it well.

"You sit on the desk and sing, so I have more room to move around when I sing to you."

He hopped up on the desk. This was fun. They always had fun together. He didn't have to try to impress her, he could just let go and be himself. No one knew him better than she did and no one knew her like he did. He knew the words to the show tunes only because he knew she liked them. He was a Rock & Roll man through and through. But then, she knew his music as well.

She sang, "If you're filled with affection, you're too shy to convey, better take my direction...feel your way." She had hip action going and a big 'come hither' look about her. On "feel your way," she took her hand and ran it down the front of her chest to her lower parts.

He stumbled on the words, but managed to recover quickly. When the song was over, he put in some Fleetwood Mac and had her hop up on the desk with him.

"Are you really thinking you might 'do it' with trombone guy? Are you really serious?"

"How serious are you about 'doing it' with boob girl?"

Moments in Time...

"She does get a rise out of me," he said looking at her sideways to see if she caught it.

"I just bet she does," she answered not quite meeting his eyes. "I think you two have gone further than we have. Not for lack of trying on trombone's part, but something is missing. I always thought my first time would be with someone I loved. Deeply." She looked sideways at him.

"I know how you feel. I always thought the same. Do you love trombone guy?"

"Do you love boob girl?"

They looked at each other and said in unison, "I only love you."

They stared at each other for a few minutes as they both came to realize what this turn of events could mean in their lives. He hopped down from the table and walked to the window. He could see his girlfriend still practicing her jumps on the mini-trampoline. He felt nothing. He turned around to face her. She was still sitting on the desk looking at him with her lips clamped shut, a nervous habit of hers. He walked to her, stood between her legs and took her hand. Again, he kissed the back. Then he kissed her cheek.

She leaned in and kissed his forehead, each eye, and very softly, kissed him on the lips. She pulled back and they stared into each other's eyes.

"I really do love only you. You are my best friend in the world and I want so very much for you to be my first." She was very red in the cheeks.

"I've loved you for so long, I don't know how we missed it. I want my first time to be with you too," he said shyly. "I know this could change everything between us," he continued.

"I know, but I love you and I want to be with you…so much it hurts."

He put in one more record. "This is the song in our game that I picked for you."

The song was 'There's a Place for Us,' from West Side Story. He stepped back between her legs and kissed her, deepening the kiss as he ran his hands through her hair. She was doing the same with him. This was the first real kiss they had shared.

They pulled back, never breaking eye contact. She pulled her shirt off, turning bright pink as she did so. She had on a see- through lace bra. He tentatively reached out and touched her there. She gasped.

"Are you okay? Did I hurt you?" But he knew he hadn't. He could see her body's response to his touch, so he ran his hand down her cheek, back to her breast, caressing her, a bold move for him, as he was very shy. "I want to keep touching you. You feel so good."

Moments in Time...

"Don't stop," she whispered. He quickly went to the door and locked it. He jogged back to her, shedding his shirt as he went.

She jumped down and removed her jeans and shoes and he did the same. About the same time, they noticed anyone looking in the window could see what was about to happen. They both put their shirts back on and removed their underwear. They never broke eye contact.

She hopped back up on the desk and he moved between her parted legs. This time there was no barrier and they were both trembling and a little breathless.

"Are you sure?" He was always a gentleman.

"Please..." was all she said looking deep into his eyes. He kissed her with all the heart he could muster. He wanted her to know how he felt about taking her virginity and giving her his.

He moved in as nature dictated. She had to scoot forward on the desk to accommodate him and she gasped again as he entered her.

"I'm sorry," he said as he stopped pushing. He had broken out in a sweat trying not to move too fast. "I love you so much, you have no idea, but I can stop if you want."

"It's okay, it's okay. I love you and I would do anything for you. Please don't stop."

In one more motion, he was all the way in. He kissed her to let her know he was aware of the emotion brewing in each of them. It was tight, but the feeling was incredible. He remained still until she gave a little nod that it was okay to keep going. She wrapped her legs around him and after a few minutes was able to move with him as he was moving in her. She arched her back as tension built inside and he put his hand against her breast and caressed her.

"Oh, God," and she said his name over and over. She clamped her legs tight around his waist and started kissing his neck.

He slowed down a little and they coninued in a slow, deep rhythm. The tension was building and their breathing was very heavy. He started kissing her deeply as he made love to the one person he knew would never fail him. She was meeting him kiss for kiss and moving with him until they both exploded.

Then they were still. He remained standing although his legs were very weak. She still had her legs around him, but he could feel her trembling. They looked each other in the eye and were overcome with emotion. She had tears running down her cheeks, but so did he.

He leaned in to kiss the tears away. They both kept giving each other soft kisses on the lips and cheeks, until he spoke.

"Are you okay? Did I hurt you?"

Moments in Time...

'It hurt a little at first and then you made it feel so good. I love feeling you inside me."

"I can't even tell you how great it felt being inside you."

"You're still inside me..." They started kissing in earnest again.

After several more minutes passed, they pulled away. They both looked at the clock and panic started setting in.

"They'll be here any minute," they said in unison.

He helped her down off the table and he could see that she had bled a little. He started to say something, but she kissed him silent. They dressed and picked up all of their things.

He spoke first in a worried tone. "We aren't virgins anymore, but are we still best friends?"

"Always," she said. "Are you sorry?"

"Never," he said. "I'm glad you were my first and I'm very glad I was yours. You know that song I'm writing? I'm writing it for you. It's supposed to be for Christmas. I still have a little way to go on it. I'm calling it 'If Only...'"

"For me? You were already thinking this might happen."

"I was dreaming it might happen, but I didn't want to lose my friend."

"I wonder where they are? This is late even for them," she said.

"Yeah, and I have a date later to feel up some huge boobs." He ducked just before she grabbed him around the neck.

She put both her hands on his shoulders. "Maybe I should go lick the window, maybe turn you on a little."

They both laughed as they left Studio D. They exited the building and walked to where the cheerleaders had been practicing. No one was around, so they walked toward the band room.

"What are we going to tell them?" She stopped walking. He kissed her cheek and took her hand in his.

"You know, things have a way of working out all by themselves. Let's just see what happens."

They saw a small group of students gathered around a window and laughing. They looked at each other and made their way over to see what was going on.

"Are you here for the show too?" A large guy pushed a smaller student out of the way so they could see in the classroom. "It happens about this time every day. You can set your watch by it."

He and she moved closer and looked in the window. They looked at each other and started laughing. Spread out on one of the science tables was trombone guy and boob girl, going at it like rabbits. He knocked on the window to get their attention and he and she both gave them a wave. Their shocked faces were a perfect Kodak moment.

He put his arm around her shoulders and she put hers around his waist. "See what I mean? Things have a way of working out for the best."

Wieland

Moments in Time...

Too Late...

He was always there. He always had been. Around every corner. Behind every door. Always watching. She couldn't even remember when she first met him. Probably early in the eighth grade. He would have been in the seventh. She couldn't drop a pencil without him showing up to get it for her. He held doors open, said please and thank you. He was quite the gentleman even at that early age. His parents had taught him well. When she sustained a broken ankle, and had to walk with crutches, he carried her books to every class. He rarely ever spoke to her. He was just always ...there. That was a very long time ago.

Eventually, he began to talk and when he did, he never stopped. She rarely had to say a word. He went on and on about any and everything. Sports, teachers, cafeteria food, his family, his religion, card games that he played at school, band, and the list goes on. It was very sweet at the time. She thought of him as a very good friend and never did anything to lead him on except talk to him. Looking back on it now, that may have been the problem.

He began to call her on the phone almost every night. The conversations were long and sometimes lasted more than two hours. During all this time and all these conversations, he never once voiced his feelings for her. She was a little naïve and a beat behind most things. She didn't see the obvious. That caused her a lot of problems in her life as she got older. When he called, and she was not home, he would talk to her mother, also for long periods of time.

Time continued to pass, as time does. The eighth grade ended, and after summer vacation, the ninth grade began. During the summer, the phone calls continued, both with her and her mother. Looking back on it, she wondered why she never thought that was strange.

With the beginning of ninth grade, a new era dawned in her life. Unfortunately, for him, it dawned in his as well. A new boy had come to the school and somehow the new boy and she, found their way to each other. Her friend was heartbroken, but he never showed any signs of it. He continued to always be present when she was not with her new boyfriend. He saw them go into a classroom one day after school and he waited until they came out. He followed them, keeping a safe distance. He knew she would tell him all about it when he called her later that night.

She knew he would call. She had been hoping her boyfriend would call, but she knew it was hard for him to do so very often. His family was large, with many brothers who would tease him unmercifully. So, when the call came, she knew who it was. Another two- hour conversation, not nearly as interesting as before, since she and her boyfriend had kissed. So, she proceeded to talk about her boyfriend, her new favorite subject. She talked of the kissing, how she felt, how he tasted, how he touched her heart. Then she said what he dreaded most. She wished it was her boyfriend she was talking to. He had imagined that he was her boyfriend. He knew it wasn't true, but he imagined it anyway.

As days turned into weeks, she told him how much she loved her boyfriend. She showed him the album she was putting together of the wedding they would have someday. He told her it was nice and that she was creative, but he told her girlfriend how jealous he was. He told her mother too. He just never told her.

After a couple more months of hearing the non-stop "I love my boyfriend. He is such a good kisser," he was beginning to think he never would have a chance with her. He told her girlfriend that 'all good things come to those who wait'. He believed that, so he continued to wait, but it was getting harder. She was no longer willing to talk for hours on the phone, but her mother and girlfriend were. They began to talk to her about how her boyfriend's family would never accept her. How they were rich and she was not. They began to fill her mind with this information. She began to wonder if what they were saying was true.

She asked her boyfriend questions and became more aggressive with him for attention. She wanted more physical contact than just kissing. She wanted to be touched. Her boyfriend tried, he really did, but he was very young. She interpreted this to mean he had lost interest in her. She started calling his house and he didn't come to the phone. He spent more time with his male friends than with her.

Looking back on this many years later, she realized he was just a boy at the time and she never knew if he even got her phone messages. She realized she had been played well by her girlfriend, her mother and by her constant shadow. She stopped eating and sleeping, problems she'd had off and on for years. She gave less and less attention to her constant companion and when she did talk to him, it was about how she couldn't live without her boyfriend. She said she would never love anyone else. At this point he'd had enough. He devised a different plan.

Her boyfriend stopped returning her calls. He appeared to be ignoring her and one day after school, after she had been filled with stories of how her boyfriend was in love with someone else, she called him. Someone on the phone told her to stop calling. He was done with her. He was breaking up and he would appreciate it if she would never speak to him again. She was with her girlfriend and her constant companion at the time, and she was not equipped to handle it. She went into hysterical sobs. She was inconsolable. Her girlfriend found two teachers who took her to the office and her girlfriend's mother picked them up. Her companion was not invited. He had struck out again. So, he continued to wait. He was sure, in time, he would have his chance.

More time passed and he was still always there. He carried her books, walked her to her classes, called her at home, but she was not the same. She stayed away from her old boyfriend. She didn't see him with any other girls, but she didn't ask questions, and honored his request to never speak to him again. And she never did.

Her companion hated seeing her like this and began to try to cheer her up by telling her another new boy in school was crazy for her. She had seen him in the band room. He played the saxophone. She admitted one day to her friend that she thought he was cute. He had blonde hair and braces and smiled all the time. He did not seem to be interested in her at all, but her girlfriend and companion continued to say it was true. She noticed them talking to him often, but would not tell her what they talked about.

Wieland

The school went on a trip to see a well- known musical at the local college. It was there that the new boy began to talk to her, at the frustration of her companion. He had done it again. Shot his own self in the foot. He saw her smile for the first time in weeks, and it was not at him. This was the start of another short- lived relationship for her, and he was once again, on the outside looking in. He couldn't understand why she never looked at him the way she had looked at her ex-boyfriend. Or this new guy. What did he have to do? Her girlfriend and her mother suspected what he was feeling, but seemed to think it was more funny than serious.

As he began to try, once again, to break this union up using the same tactics he had used before, he found out something very interesting. She did not have the depth of feeling for this boy that she had for the first. She rarely kissed him and when she did, there was no passion like he had seen with the first. He found he had to do very little in the way of keeping them apart, because the new boy's mother disapproved of her right away. She was not good enough for her son. One day after school, the new boyfriend told her he could not see her anymore. She was very hurt, but was expecting it. Then his mother showed up and told her just how wrong she was for her son. It was an ugly speech. When it was over, she nodded once, turned around and left.

He was still always there. Ready to pick up the pieces. But he was full of guilt about his part in causing

Moments in Time...

her problems. Her girlfriend was feeling guilty as well and was afraid to apologize, so everything was swept under the rug. The only thing that was said from her girlfriend was that she realized now how much her friend had been in love with her first boyfriend. Her girlfriend offered to talk to her ex-boyfriend but she told her no. She had made a decision that once someone had broken up with her, she would never go back. Her constant companion was sure that now he stood a chance. But he still did not say anything about his feelings and she still had not realized what he felt for her.

As the school year went on, he continued to be near her. Always teasing her and calling her stupid names trying to get her attention. The harder he tried, the more she shut down. She threw herself into her school work and work on the stage, band, and choir. As the school year came to an end, he saw that her feelings for him were still no more than friendship. He stopped calling her as often and when he did, the calls were less than fifteen minutes. He stopped calling her mother and her girlfriend. He knew it was time to give up. But he was not going down without a fight.

When the next school year began, they were all in the high school in the next town. He avoided her and took classes that were in a different location than the ones she was involved in. She had no contact with him or her ex-boyfriend. What she did find out was that she was very popular with boys in the grade below her. She was asked for her phone number a lot, taken to the movies where she made out and was occasionally felt up by these boys.

But it didn't last long. Only until they asked for sex, which was usually after one date. She would be shocked and turn them down. Finally, one boy spilled the beans. Her phone number was on the wall in the boy's bathroom saying to call for a good time. A few boys ratted out her old companion as having told them the same thing. She was crushed. She felt like it was her fault. She couldn't find him to ask what he had been thinking. He didn't take her phone calls. He was not home when she went by his house. She just didn't know why he would do such a thing. She finally had to let it go.

A few years later, when she was in college, she received a call from her old friend. He was in the Navy, and home on leave. He asked if he could see her. She was thrilled and agreed. He came to pick her up and he had grown very tall. Nice looking as well. Totally different than the old friend he had been in junior high. He took her for ice cream and they talked about how much their lives had changed. He apologized for what he had done by telling the boys she was easy. She forgave him. She was looking at him in a new way. Feelings were stirring that she had not had before. The same was happening for him. He decided to take her for

Moments in Time...

a drive on the Parkway in their town, and he found a secluded spot with trees, which was rare in that area.

As he parked the car, he turned to look at her. She looked at him in a way she had not done before.

"Why did you do that to me with the other boys? You were such a good friend to me all through junior high."

He looked her in the eye. "I wasn't such a good friend. Not like you think."

"I don't understand," she replied.

He confessed to all he had done to plant seeds of doubt in her and her first boyfriend's head. Her first boyfriend had not had another girlfriend. With her next boyfriend, he really had not done much. That boyfriend's mother really had been against her being in her son's life.

She was still confused. "Why did you do all those things? You were always there for me. I thought you were a good friend."

He looked at her and with a red face confessed. "I loved you. I wanted you to love me and be my girlfriend. I always did. But I didn't know how to tell you. I was afraid after your first boyfriend, you would never look at me that way."

"You never said. You should have. It might have been different." She was a little breathless. "You never contacted me in high school."

"I was too ashamed of what I had done. I had to let go. I was almost obsessed". He was becoming breathless too. "I'm saying it now. I love you. I always have."

Who moved first, neither of them knew. Both seemed more experienced. She thought it would be nice to make out with someone who had been around and knew what he was doing. They kissed deeply, over and over. Their lips and tongues met and she experienced feelings she didn't know she had. She was so breathless she could barely speak.

"We should have done this a long time ago. It feels right. Does it feel right to you too?"

"It feels right. It wouldn't have felt right years ago." He was out of breath. "The timing is better now."

She wanted him. Here. Now. She didn't want to think of the consequences or anything but him. He wanted her, too. He unbuttoned her shirt and unclasped her bra while he continued kissing her. His hands moved over her breasts. She groaned and told him not to stop. He didn't. He replaced his hands with his mouth and she had sensations like never before. She moved her hand to give him some pleasure too. He gasped.

Moments in Time...

"Let's get out of the car. I have a blanket in the trunk. No one can see us under these pine trees."

He could barely formulate the words he was so out of breath and she could barely stand when she left the car. He spread out the blanket over pine needles and helped her lie down. He just noticed how thin and fit she had become. He took her clothes off and his own. He began kissing her again on the lips, on the neck leaving a mark there, and on her breasts, leaving a mark there as well. She could feel his arousal and she had never felt or seen that before. She started to shake, but knew she would not stop. She would think about the consequences tomorrow.

They both broke out in a sweat and the activity stopped for a moment. She did not know how to proceed but was sure he did. He looked at her and told her she was so beautiful. He softly ran his fingers over the tips of her breasts causing her to cross her legs, she was so excited. He moved his hands across her lower abdomen and between her legs giving her pleasure for the first time. Then he moved his fingers a little lower into her secret place and she said that it hurt. He tried again and she still said it hurt. He pulled his hand away and rolled over on his back. She could see he didn't want to stop. He'd probably had plenty of girls in the Navy. She figured she must not measure up.

He looked at her. "I can't do this right now. You are beautiful and I love you, but there are too many unknowns. We have no protection. I could be shipped out any day now. It would be wrong."

"Okay," she said. "Will I hear from you?"

"Of course, as soon as I know where I will be. I won't lose you again." He kissed both her breasts one last time, pulled on his pants and gave her some privacy to dress. He had gone to stand a distance away from the other side of the car. She wondered what he could be doing. She was always a beat behind, even back in those days. He drove her home and kissed her as much as he could before he drove away. She felt happy. Like things were as they should be.

She waited for several months without any word from him. After ten months had passed, she had to let it go. Maybe it had been payback for years ago when she didn't return his feelings. She met another young man and threw caution to the wind, giving herself and marrying him all in six quick weeks.

Three years later, after she'd had a son, she was visiting her mother and the subject of her old friend came up. She told her mother that she always wondered what had happened to him after the last time he had visited.

"I wasn't supposed to say anything, but he came by here about a year and a half ago with a ring to ask you to marry him." Her mother looked away from her shocked face.

Moments in Time...

"Why didn't you tell me? Why didn't he call me?" She was very upset.

"Because you were already married. I told him he should have called after the last time he was here and he said he was shipped out right away. The med cruise, to which he was assigned, was extended twice. He knew he should have called or written, but he thought you'd wait." She continued changing her new grandson and turned away from her daughter. "I just told him he was too late."

Six years passed and she was into her second marriage, and living in a very small town a little north of where they grew up. She was in the little Mom and Pop store in the area looking to rent a movie. He was there too. She called his name. He turned around and grabbed her in a big hug. They spoke like old friends, telling each other what was going on in their lives. He was married and working as a detective in the town in which they grew up. He had to get going but promised to keep in touch.

It was almost twenty years before she heard from him again. She had joined a high school site on the internet and the day after, he contacted her. She was on her third marriage and he was on his second. He was teaching school in one of the southern states but was going to have to go to his home town to close down his old house. His father had passed away some time back. They e-mailed back and forth for a couple of weeks and it was clear there were still feelings on both their parts. The e-mails became more personal and he told her why he had stopped caressing her that time on the Parkway. That had been his very first kiss and first carnal knowledge of any girl. He had assumed she'd had lovers since high school and when he'd found that she was still a virgin, he'd panicked. He didn't want to leave her high and dry if she became pregnant. As to why he never called her, he said he just thought she'd wait.

He confessed about showing up to ask her to marry him and that he had told her mother not to tell her and interrupt her life. He asked her to come to town. He could use a friend and would like a chance to pick up where they had left off. They had some racy e-mail exchanges and she just didn't feel right about the whole thing. She said she would e-mail her answer in a couple of days.

After a week had passed, when he was already in his home town, she received this one simple e-mail from him.

"I know. You don't have to answer. Once again I am too late..."

Moments in Time...

Once in a Lifetime

He had been outside tending to the flower beds that were so important to her, in another lifetime. He wiped the sweat from his brow and with an unsteady gait, walked into the sitting room where he could watch her. She was sitting in her rocker, handmade by him, staring out the window as was her custom at this time of day.

He sat in his easy chair and closed his weary eyes. He remembered the day he first laid eyes on her over forty- one years ago. She was beautiful in spirit. A real lady. She had been a visitor at his church. The church he had attended most of his life, as had his parents and grandparents before him. She had been with some vague acquaintances that he had only spoken to a few times. He could not even remember their names. How he had wished he had paid more attention to those around him.

Wieland

She looked at him and the connection was instant. He slowly walked in her direction, his eyes never moving from hers, and when he reached her, she took his hand and introduced herself. She seemed to be aware that he did not know her friends even though they were a part of the same church. She was intuitive that way and she had not wanted to embarrass him.

From that day on, they had been an item. Spending time together, laughing, loving, and eventually marrying. She had been a teacher in the local school and he had made a living as a salesman at the local furniture store. On the side, he did carpentry, making some beautiful pieces of furniture that he sold as custom work for those in his small town.

When the time came, they started a family. Two sons and a daughter. After their first child was born, she stopped working to stay at home and raise her family. That was how things had been in the old days. Not so much anymore. Now it took both husband and wife working outside the home just to make ends meet.

They had lost their daughter to polio when she was eight years old. His wife had been devastated for months and he had taken on the raising of the two boys. But her faith had always been strong and she pulled through. Life went on as usual, for the boys and for him.

As the boys grew into strong men, they had been drafted into the war. Their oldest son never made it back home, having been killed in action by friendly fire

Moments in Time...

as it were. That had been a bitter pill to swallow for them both and it was several years before life returned to normal. Their younger son married and raised a family of his own halfway across the country. They received pictures of their grandchildren and letters from their son and daughter in law, but they would have loved to have been closer to them. So, as they began the golden years of their lives together, it was just the two of them, just as they had started out.

She was still beautiful in spirit and strong in her faith. He wished he was as resilient as she back in the day. They moved out to the country where they had a vegetable garden and a flower garden as well. Gardening was her specialty and her vegetables always placed in the county fair each year, sometimes winning the top prize. She loved to garden, almost as much as he loved his carpentry work. They took ballroom dancing lessons together and he had to say, they made a dashing couple on the dance floor. They had many friends and their church family as well, but enjoying each other had been what they loved most.

Sadly, as they grew older, life had started to become more difficult. They developed some health issues, he with heart problems and she with her memory. At first it was little things with her forgetting the mail or to pick up the dry cleaning. Then one day she left the stove on and a small fire started. She had been asleep in another room at the time and nearly died of smoke inhalation.

He, on the other hand, would take care of himself for a while and then revert back to old habits that were better off left alone. She had kept him on track until she could no longer do so. His body was failing, but his mind was strong. Her body was strong but her mind was failing.

The thing that never changed was the love he had for her. He would have done anything to change the course that her life had taken. Watching the light dwindle out of her eyes, and as the disease progressed, the change in her personality was almost more than he could bear. She became combative at times not knowing who he was. He thought that was the hardest to understand and live with. Still, he took the best care he could of her. They had been together for forty years and had promised to love one another until death would part them.

He opened his eyes and knew right away that something was different. She was looking at him. Her eyes, that were usually blank, were alive with memories, with promises, with hope. He slowly stood and walked toward her. When he was at her side, she took his hand, never looking away from him. His heart swelled with emotion. Still holding her hand, he helped her to stand. She was still beautiful. He picked her up and carried her into the room they had shared these last forty years. He laid her on the bed covered in the quilt she had so painstakingly made the first year of their marriage. She looked at him with tears in her eyes and

Moments in Time...

said his name. He took his hand and smoothed the hair from her face as he gathered her close to his heart.

"It is time," she said.

He kissed her lips and she touched his face. In that brief moment, he understood the true meaning of making love. His soul was on fire with love for this woman, his wife, his best friend. He could feel her spirit leaving and he knew the moment when she was gone. He closed her eyes and knew his life would change forever, but nothing could ever take away the life they had shared. It was real and true and forever branded in his heart and soul.

He felt tears run down his face and put his cheek to hers. She had a single tear that had leaked from her eye as well and he felt some kind of comfort as their tears blended together. Just like their love and their lives had done. She was gone and he did not know how he would carry on.

He felt a heaviness descend upon him and at the same time a lightening of his spirit. He was not sure what it meant but he knew all was well. He took her face in his hands and kissed her one last time. He lay back on the bed next to her and breathed his last. And their love was united forever in spirit and in truth just as they had lived their lives for all those years. A love that comes along once in a lifetime.

Wieland

Although I have never told him, this story was inspired by Richard Diakun and the forever love he has for his darling wife of thirty plus years, Lisa. Although the bodies may fade away one day, this kind of love lives on, unceasing in it's quest inside the heart and the soul. And with that, it breathes life forever.

Moments in Time...

The Call

The ringing of the phone was starting to get on his nerves. Someone had called twice earlier without leaving a message and the caller ID said 'name unavailable'. He hated that. If someone wanted to talk to him bad enough to call, then they should at least have the decency to leave a message. Any one that really knew him, knew that he would be watching this game tonight. At least he was trying to watch it.

It was funny how the ringing phone didn't bother his wife. She carried her phone in her pocket and always answered it when it rang. During dinner, during work, during his discussion of the political candidates, during...well, he wouldn't go there. She had a knack for knowing if the call was important or not. Sometimes she could even tell who was on the phone. She had quite a gift, but then, she was gifted in a lot of ways. That is why he was still married to her after thirty years. Not the only reason, but one of the top five. Her kindness to others and to himself was probably number one.

It couldn't be that easy to live with him on a daily basis. Not that he was a bad guy. Not at all. He had lots of friends, but he had his own interests as well. And she had hers. They allowed each other space to be themselves and did not require an explanation for every little thing they did. He had his music, which he loved. Sometimes it consumed him, but she didn't complain. Now that he thought about it, she hadn't been all that interested lately. He would have to think about that later.

Damn! His mind was wandering and he had missed an important play. And there goes the phone again. He picked it up. Same thing on the caller ID. He put the phone back down and put a cushion over it for good measure.

"I think you should answer it. The ring sounds like it could be someone who just needs a friend."

"Now? Really? Why now?" He looked at her face and saw she was very serious. He had a feeling that maybe she was right.

"Hello," he said as cordially as possible, after all they were interrupting the game.

Silence. Strange. He could hear someone breathing.

Again, he spoke. "Hello."

Moments in Time...

He could hear a sniffling sound, like whomever the caller was, had a cold. His wife had wandered over and she had a worried look on her face. He was about to hang up thinking it was a prank call, but she stopped him.

"You need to keep trying. I think something is wrong." Then she turned the television off.

He made a grab for the remote but she kept it out of his reach and gestured that he should continue to try to communicate with the caller.

"I'm sorry for interrupting the game," said the caller. "I know how important it is to you."

"Oh, hi, how are you? I was thinking about you earlier today. I meant to call, but you know how it is with work and the wife." He rolled his eyes and ducked just in time to keep from getting hit with the dog's toy that had been thrown at him. He put his hand over the phone and mouthed to her that it was a friend from work. Nothing to worry about.

"You know I don't know how it is. My wife left me six months ago and today I got my pink slip at work," said the caller. "So come Monday morning, I won't be in the cubicle next to you. It is the end of an era, the end of a lot of things."

"I am so sorry. I had no idea. Did you have any indication this was coming?" His wife sat on the end of the sofa still keeping the remote well away from him.

Wieland

"I've missed a few assignments and shown up late a few times, well, more than a few times. I guess it wasn't a total shock, but I thought I could pull out of the funk I've been in before the big bosses noticed."

He knew his friend had been struggling with the breakup of his marriage. They had been married for twenty years and his children were avoiding him as well.

"Hey," he said looking at his wife for confirmation. "How about coming over and watching the game here? We can have a blast rooting for the opposite teams. Come on, it'll help get your mind off things for a while." He heard his friend swallowing something and it hit him that his friend's voice was a little slurred. Why didn't he notice that before? His bad feeling just got worse.

"I can't come over. I'm really calling only to say goodbye to one of the nicest friends and co-workers that I have ever had. You took me under your wing when I first came to work with you and covered for me more times than you should have when my work wasn't up to par."

"You're starting to scare me. How about if I come over there? My wife will send some of her famous trail mix. Homemade. I know you love that." Again, he looked to his wife for confirmation. She just nodded.

"Please say goodbye to your wife for me and tell her that she is very lucky to have you for a husband."

"What do you mean? Where are you going? Stop talking this way. It's not funny in the least."

Moments in Time...

"No, it's not and I'm probably going to Hell for it, but that has to be better than this empty existence." The words were getting more slurred by the minute.

"Are you saying what I think you're saying? How much have you had to drink?"

"Almost a fifth of Vodka and several sleeping pills. And if that doesn't work, I have a loaded Glock 20 waiting for the right moment."

"No!" He jumped up. "You can't do this. I have to call someone. I'll be right over. I'm going to call 911. I'll get you some help and stay with you as long as it takes!" He looked at his wife and she was already gathering up his wallet and car keys.

"No, man. If I see any of the authorities, I'll put a bullet in my head. Just let me go to sleep. I only called to say goodbye."

He thought a minute and issued up a prayer for the right words to say. "No, you didn't call to say good bye." He took a deep breath. "You called for help. Remember the time when you helped me through some health issues when, frankly, I didn't know if I was going to make it? Then there was that time when the tree fell on our roof. You were the one to help me repair the damage. No one else showed up. And...and..." He was running out the door and gesturing to his wife to call for help.

"Be careful," she yelled. "I'll handle things with the authorities."

He squealed tires as he began to make the fifteen-minute drive to his friend's house.

"Are you still there? I'm on my way. We'll figure this out. I promise. Don't do anything else." He knew he had to keep him talking.

"How about that time when I was in the hospital and my wife was sick? You came to sit with me during the procedure I was having. You knew I was nervous. Then you went to my house and brought soup and rolls so my wife would have something to eat. She was too weak to prepare anything for herself. You gave us both moral support when you didn't have to. You are a very worthwhile person. Please don't make me lose my friend. Please. I'm almost there."

His friend's words were barely audible. "I love you man...keep the faith..."

His tires screeched to a halt in front of his friend's house. He heard nothing further on the phone but he was afraid to hang up. Then he heard a gunshot that nearly deafened him. He dropped the phone and ran to the door. It was locked. He started banging on it without any response from his friend. Where was the help that was supposed to be here? He looked under the doormat. There was the key. He was afraid to enter, but he had to. For his friend.

He called his name when he was in the house and slowly made his way to the bedroom. There was his friend lying across the bed. The gun was by his lifeless hand, but there was no blood. Anywhere. He felt for a pulse and found it was very weak and rapid. He had made it in time! His body sagged and he sat on the bed in relief.

The police and ambulance arrived next and as they tried to revive his friend he thought back on the evenings events. Had he done enough? If it hadn't been for his wife, he would not have taken the call. She had been a blessing to him and to his friend. Maybe saved his friend's life.

As the ambulance rolled his friend out of the house, his friend's eyes opened and he reached out to him. "I knew I called the right person." His voice was just a whisper. "I shot the gun so I wouldn't accidentally shoot anyone else. Thank you. I do need help and you knew it too." He closed his eyes as they loaded him into the ambulance.

As the ambulance pulled away, and he had answered all the questions from the authorities, he found his cell phone and called his wife.

"I got there in time. He is on the way to the hospital and he was able to acknowledge that he needs help. I will be there for him every step of the way. Thank you for making me answer the phone."

"I just had a feeling that it was important and that you would be able to help. Thank you for not arguing.

Wieland

You have earned the right to have the remote back. Now let me tell you about the game..."

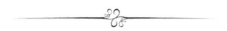

This story was inspired by Lisa Diakun and is dedicated to her as she forever lives in the hearts of her loving family and devoted husband, Richard.

Moments in Time...

Reconciliation

She sat silently in her living room in the home she had maintained for more years than she could remember. Since her youngest son was still at home and that was over forty years ago. Where had all the time gone? Too many years, too many hurts, too many lives shaped by the past. Years that could never be recovered. She continued to sit in silence pondering the past and the future.

She had been to the doctor that morning and had received news that would change her world forever. Not what she wanted to hear. She was independent. She'd had to be. With five children to feed, she and her husband had both had to work outside the home to make ends meet. Then when the divorce happened, she was still left with the two youngest boys. The older of the two not staying long before he joined the military. For several years, it was just her and the youngest.

She'd had to make hard choices throughout her life. Most decisions had been left to her to make and she was not always the best one to make them. Conversation with her spouse had been difficult, with most issues never resolved, especially concerning the children. And with her spouse working long, hard hours, most of the discipline was left to her as well. She had let herself become hard, and inflexible during their formative years. She took offense easily, even when her children were young, but especially so after the divorce.

The children tended to side with their father. This caused her great distress. She felt she had been the parent giving the most to raise them without a lot of help from the father. *How could they side with him and leave her to have to defend herself without any real ammunition to do so? How could they?* She felt a moment of great resentment rise up in her, similar to the resentment she had carried all these years wondering why she didn't count for much in the eyes of her children.

She wasn't deluded about the situation. She knew she had caused a lot of the problems herself by building the walls she had built in order to cope. She felt her children had deserted her. Even the youngest. She knew he couldn't wait to get away from her as well, and would do so as soon as he was old enough. And he did. He was younger by several years than the next oldest boy. He was her last child. The one the others found pleasure in tormenting. She should have done more to stop that,

Moments in Time...

but she had felt it was normal sibling rivalry. If she could only turn back time. But it was too late. She had burned her bridges.

Now as she sat in her home that she loved, she had to face the fact that her life was coming to an end. The doctor had said that another bout of pneumonia could do her in. Maybe even another fall. She'd had both, several times in the past few years. She had trouble admitting those facts, even now that the end was in sight. The doctor had spoken of getting her affairs in order and of hospice. She was a nurse. She had been a nurse for nearly forty years before she retired. She knew what 'getting her affairs in order' and 'going on hospice' meant.

Over the years, periodically, one of her children would come around. Different ones at different times. However, it never lasted long. Either she would offend them or they would offend her and any chance of a real relationship was lost before it even began. Except for her youngest son. He had forced a relationship upon her against her will, she was sad to admit, about seven or eight years ago. It had been a rocky relationship as they were a lot alike in hanging on to issues of the past. She admired him, though. He had taken on the task of taking care of his mother in law with Alzheimer's disease. He had been doing it with his wife for more than six years now.

She wanted to believe that she had a hand in raising him to be this kind of man. He had also tried to get her to consider moving in with he and his wife, so that he could take care of her as well when the time came. But she felt that would be detrimental to his home and to herself. They had too many battles to be living under the same roof. He did, however, call almost every day, even when she never returned his calls. He visited often and did minor repairs and improvements around her house, again, against her will most of the time. Most of the things he worked on or set up proved to be of benefit to her, and she had ended up being grateful after all.

Time continued to pass, as it does, and she began the process of wrapping up her life in paperwork with her attorney. Her youngest daughter made an attempt to help her with some of those affairs but she decided to leave her final disposition of her estate to a friend from her church and to her niece. She also had her youngest son act as her medical power of attorney.

She had trouble sleeping at night thinking about all that had been done and said with her different children. The oldest son and daughter were a lot like her. Inflexible and holding on to the past. She saw a lot of herself in them and wished somehow they would find it in their hearts to learn to forgive, even though she had not attained that herself. She knew time was running out and she did not have long left in this world to at least make a difference with her children. So, she decided, during a conversation with her youngest son, to make

Moments in Time...

an effort with each of her children to make amends and when the time came, to have her family with her.

She became worse sooner than she would have thought and had to be hospitalized. During the stay at the hospital, she was forced to realize she could no longer remain in her home. Upon discharge, she was placed in an assisted living facility, never to live in her home again. Her friends and youngest son helped get her house and belongings packed up and ready to be sold.

She had decided while she had been in the hospital that she would forgive and let go of all the old hurts and offenses that she had built up inside over the many years. This was probably the hardest thing she had ever done. Understanding that forgiveness is a choice, love is a choice, offenses can only hurt us if we let them. She wrote a letter to each of her children trying to explain her love for them, apologizing for all the hurt she had caused and asked for their forgiveness. She asked that they come to a special estate sale of her belongings before the public was invited in. None of them came except her youngest son.

She continued to decline without hearing anything from her children. As she became bedridden and her heart needed more and more oxygen just to keep beating, she realized her children would not forgive her. She didn't even know her grandchildren and now it was too late. If only she could go back and do things differently. Hindsight and all, you know? She had always felt she had done the best she could at the time for each of her children. But now the lesson she had learned was this. *Measure your words carefully before you speak, because once spoken, they can never be unspoken.* How she wished things could have been different.

Time had run out. She was barely able to breathe. She struggled with each breath even with her oxygen turned up as high as possible. She was given medication by the hospice nurses to try to keep her comfortable. She had made peace with her Lord and Savior, but her anxiety still remained. She had one friend by her side and was unable to even talk to her youngest on the phone. Later, he would tell his wife that he'd had a feeling he should have gone to be with her that morning.

She didn't want the medicine they kept giving her. She was holding out, hoping her prayers would be answered and her children would come to be with her in her final moments. As her eyes were closing against her will, she heard the door open and in walked her oldest son with his family. She fought the tranquilizer flowing through her veins, prayed for it to be rendered useless for just a little while. Her son walked over to her and took her hand. He said, "I'm sorry, mom." No other words were necessary. She tried to speak but the strength to do so was gone. He understood. She could see it in his eyes.

Moments in Time...

The door opened again and her oldest daughter was by her side. Again, no words were necessary. She took her mother's hand in hers and brought it to her cheek. She could feel her daughter's tears and managed through gasping breaths to speak.

"I'm so sorry."

Behind her oldest daughter she could see her other daughter and son. One at a time they sat at her side and held her hand. She managed a last 'I love you' to them all and thought of her youngest son and knew he was there with her in spirit. The Lord had answered her prayer. She could let go now. The old hurts were gone and replaced by love and forgiveness.

Her breathing slowed and her eyes closed for the last time. Her children began to softly sing 'Amazing Grace'. Her life drifted away surrounded by her family at last. After all, isn't this how you would like it to be on your deathbed?

This story is dedicated to my late mother-in-law, Ella Mae Wieland, and was the outcome she had wanted for her family. I promised her I would write it.

Wieland

Moments in Time...

The Scene

How was it that every time he was in a crowd of people, he still managed to feel totally alone. It wasn't that no one would talk to him, just a feeling that when they did, he wasn't really there in their eyes. He'd had too much to drink already trying to get up the courage to speak to a girl from his History class. He wasn't a drinker, but his nerves were getting the best of him.

He walked over to her. "Hi. I'm in your History class. I was a little high during class yesterday, so can I borrow your notes?" He winked at her and looked her up and down. After all, isn't that what girls were looking for?

"Lookin' good," he said.

"No, you may not borrow my notes, asshole." She flung her long hair in his face and marched herself in the other direction.

He tried to look around to see if anyone was a witness to his 'crash and burn'. *What was he thinking? He didn't get high.* He noticed a few girls looking his way and laughing. Forget it. He was just going to go home. He clearly wasn't cut out for this scene. On the way out, he grabbed another cup of the spiked punch and slugged it down. *One for the road, he thought.* He noticed the girl behind the punch table. She was looking at him with a smile on her pretty face. He started to say something, but changed his mind. *What was the point? He'd just get shot down again.*

He got as far as the curb before he had to sit down. Things were looking a little hazy. His vision wasn't clear at all and his mind was going in and out of focus. *Ha! In and out. Damn! He was going to be a virgin forever at this rate.*

He backed up a little on the grass and tried to find a good spot to lie back. He was partially concealed by some large pine trees. Stargazing. He'd always liked that. He'd like it better if he had someone to share it with.

"Hey, handsome. I've been watching you."

He looked up to see the pretty girl from the punch table. Long blonde hair, big green eyes, legs that he would just love to get a better look at. She was wearing a short denim skirt and a shirt that was low cut and had buttons down the front. God, she was gorgeous. *She must have him mixed up with someone else.*

Moments in Time...

She sat beside him and put her hand on his leg, running it up to his growing...imagination. Hell of a time to be a virgin.

She unbuttoned her shirt just enough to tease him with her see-through bra. He was becoming quite aroused.

"Just go with it, baby, take my lead. No one can see us here."

She ran her hands up his tee shirt pulling it over his head and ran her fingernails down his chest causing goosebumps all over his body. Then she began to kiss him like butterflies all over his chest. It felt so good that he was afraid that he might have an accident in his pants. *God, he'd die if that happened.*

She leaned forward and kissed him on his lips. "I've been wanting to do that ever since I saw you enter the room earlier."

She took kissing to a whole new level. He had kissed girls before but never like this. She took off her shirt and unzipped his pants. She touched him where no girl had at this time in his life.

"Nice, baby, real nice. How about I show you how to use that?"

All he could do was nod.

She moved to position herself over him and undid the front clasp of her bra.

Wieland

"Touch me," she said as she guided him in the best way to please her. She put her hands over his.

"That's what I like."

She began to show him things that he had only seen before in magazines and movies. He was losing it fast. She continued kissing and touching him in forbidden places until he thought he would surely pass out.

"Give me your hand," she said, and proceeded to suck two of his fingers into her mouth. She sat just to the side of him and let her legs fall apart, once again teaching him things he had only dreamed about.

She was caught up in the heat of the moment as much as he was and he watched as she rode the waves of her own pleasure.

When she was past her point of no return, she turned her attention back to him and his needs. She began to kiss his neck as she claimed his virginity with all the enthusiasm that an experienced teenaged girl could manage.

His eyes crossed. Nothing had ever felt this good and he was afraid it never would again. She slowly took her time with him even though she had to know this couldn't possibly last long. His breath was coming in gasps. So was hers. Sensation had been building and then, it was over.

Spent, they both lay back on the grass. She leaned over and kissed him deeply and he kissed her back just as eagerly. They were both drenched in sweat. He leaned over her and kissed her neck and ears using his tongue, hoping to give her half the pleasure she had given him. She tasted so good. She had enjoyed the activity as much as he and he felt very proud of himself. Then he woke up.

Wieland

Moments in Time...

Come and Get It

"If you want it, here it is, come and get it..." He was singing to himself while he was looking in the mirror. He was gorgeous, if he did say so himself. Who wouldn't want it? He couldn't imagine a girl, woman, or even some men who wouldn't want it. Not that he was into men. He wasn't, but he enjoyed their looks of envy and of interest as well.

As he continued to gaze at himself he said out loud to no one in particular, "What's not to like?"

He was tall. He was buff. He had washboard abs and was a blonde 'Adonis' as he had heard himself described on more than one occasion. His eyes were 'cornflower blue' as one girl had described them. Another had said she could see 'forever' in his eyes. Now that was corny, even for him. He was proud of his eyelashes, though. Very long, very thick, and very hot.

Wieland

He turned around and took a hand- held mirror so he could admire his sexy backside. *Yeah, baby! It doesn't come any better than this!* His jeans hugged every inch of his body, like they had been painted on. They accentuated his body quite nicely and his designer shirt was open halfway down his hairless chest. He had no equal in the looks department.

"Are you looking at your own backside again?" His sister was standing just outside the bathroom door with a look of disgust on her face.

"You're just jealous because I got all the good looks in the family. Sorry you missed out. That's what happens when you're born after the face of greatness."

He knew she hated it when he referred to his status as her elder, even though only two years separated them. He liked to tease her about her looks when, in truth, she was a 'hottie' as much as he was. But, as his little sister, she cramped his style.

"Get out of the bathroom, you jerk, and let someone else have a turn." She barged in on him, but he was ready for a night on the town anyway, so he let her get away with it.

"I just don't see what the girls see in you, or the women, and even the old gals. I just don't get it." She looked him up and down. "No, still don't get it."

"You don't have to get it. I have enough females getting it already and you'd be at the end of a very…long…line." He bent over to look her straight in the face when he said this.

"Ewww…that's just gross, even for you." She pushed him out of the bathroom.

"Idiot!" She yelled through the door at him. "One day someone is going to turn the tables on you and you are going to be some kind of sorry for all the females you've screwed over."

She stared at herself in the mirror. Not too bad. Her hair was a darker shade of blonde than his, but she had to admit, he was right about his looks. She smiled as she thought, *he might get his comeuppance sooner than he thinks. You just never know!* She grabbed her cell phone and headed down the stairs.

He had about four main hangouts that he frequented depending on his mood for the evening. Tonight, he was in the mood for the 'high-end stuck up' chicks. They could be a challenge sometimes because they were usually looking for older, more professional looking men. He looked younger than his twenty- six years, but he could move and talk in a much sexier manner than the men they were seeking. He loved beautiful women, plain women, older women, younger women, women of all kinds, and even dated the occasional charity case if he was feeling generous. He could not, however, date the ugly, hairy, sweaty, nasty smelling really fat chicks. Oh, he wasn't above flirting with them, but that's where he drew the line.

He set himself a challenge for the evening. He planned to have a date with the hottest chick in the place in, oh, twenty minutes. He ambled up to the bar with that swagger of his. He ordered a shot of tequila and a beer chaser and downed them both. He surveyed the room until he found the lucky lady. He could tell the eyes of almost everyone in the bar were upon him. He saw a few girls that he had dated in the past and could tell they hoped to be the lucky ones tonight. Maybe, if he couldn't find 'the one' he would let one or two of them have a hot make out session with him. That was always fun.

Finally, he saw the one he wanted. Five minutes had passed. She was sitting at the end of the long bar stirring her drink with an olive on a swizzle stick. Probably a dry martini and he would be willing to bet she was unhappy about something. Probably a boyfriend that had not treated her as she felt she should have been treated.

"Hi, sunshine," he said as he leaned on the bar next to her.

She gave him a 'go to Hell' look and turned in the other direction. Not one to give up easily, he moved to the other side to try again.

Moments in Time...

"You look so sad, beautiful. Is there anything I can do to help? A shoulder to cry on perhaps? I'm a great listener." He moved his hand to tuck her long dark hair behind her ear. He casually brushed his finger down her cheek. She looked sideways at him and he could see unshed tears ready to fall. He knew he had her.

He liked this place because it had a unisex bathroom. All he had done was put his arms around her.

"Everything will be okay, beautiful, and if it's not, I'm always around."

She had kissed him first so he knew this was going to be good. Revenge sex, if he got that lucky, was some of the best he had ever had. He guided her to the small table in the room and sat her on it, kissing her deeply all the while. She was kissing him back just as deeply. He tentatively put his hand on her breast, caressing her, while she was running her fingers through his hair.

"Let me show you how it feels to be with the best." He leaned into her and he knew she could tell he was aroused by her touch.

"This had better be the best time of my life." She looked him in the eye as she said it.

"It will be, baby, it will be. I can promise you that." He continued to kiss and caress her as much as she would allow.

Wieland

She was begging for it, and he was just the one to give it to her.

"If you want it, here it is, come and get it..." He sang as he ran his fingers through her hair. "Do you want it, baby?"

"Yes! But will you respect me afterwards? Will you call me?"

"Of course I will. Someone as beautiful and sexy as you? Come on, how could I not?"

He had her lay back on the table and gave her exactly what she asked for. And he just had to say, he had been magnificent. A true master of the art.

When it was over, he kissed her thoroughly and told her she was the best he had ever had and she agreed, he was the best as well. He had to admit, she was good. In the top ten anyway.

They returned to the bar and he sprang for another drink for her, told her he would call her and left her sitting there, much as he had found her. However, she looked a lot happier. But then, who wouldn't, having been with someone who was as awesome as he?

As he left the bar, he could tell some of his regular girls were upset that he had passed them up. *Oh, well,*

who cares anyway, he thought. He could get any girl he wanted. He was feeling good and strutting down the street singing his song.

"If you want it, here it is, come and get it…"

"I want it, lover," he heard someone say.

"Me, too," said another voice.

"Is that right." It was a statement, not a question. He had seen them around. Always together. They were young, but he was sure they were at least over eighteen. One had shoulder length red hair and the other was a platinum blonde with short 'messy' hair. Very pretty with nice legs. He could do this.

"Let's go to another place. One we've seen you in before," said the redhead. "It's only two blocks over, you know the place. The bathroom is nice. There is a love seat that is comfortable. And it has a chair for nursing mothers. It's like our own private room for our own private party. We can have a good time in there."

"Ditto, that," said the blonde. "My aunt runs the place, so she won't let us be disturbed and we might get drinks on the house."

Okay. He knew the manager. Ugliest woman he had ever seen. Over six feet tall and three hundred pounds easily. Lots of black hair all over her arms and legs. Even the face and…well, everywhere. When he first met her, he couldn't tell if she was male or female. But he liked to keep on the good side of management, so he flirted with her from time to time. He knew she wanted him too by the way she gave him a hug every time he came in the place. One time she had walked in on him making out with two older gals. She asked if she could join them and he had told her maybe another time, but he had never taken her up on it.

He started singing his song as they walked to the other bar. The two girls linked arms with him and sang loudly. He wasn't totally comfortable with that since it was, after all, his song. They were tone deaf, but if he wanted to party with them, he had better shut his pie hole.

As they entered the upscale bar, he noticed a girl he had dated last week was there. No angry eyes from her that he could tell. As they passed her, he was sure she had winked at him. Could he handle three? Of course, he could, but the girl didn't look all that interested. She was talking to someone on her other side that looked like...no it couldn't be his...no not here. He turned that thought off right now. He saw the manager, who blew him a kiss and he gave her a wave and a wink. She winked back and pointed her finger from herself to him. He just laughed and hoped she didn't interrupt.

They went into the bathroom and the two girls got comfortable on the love seat.

"We saw you come out of the bathroom at the other bar with that prissy bitch and we've heard you're the best date around. Think you can handle making out with the both of us?"

"Maybe if you get me warmed up a little first. I mean, I'm the best, but I was just with someone thirty minutes ago." He was flexing his muscles and giving them a good view of his spectacular body.

"Not a problem," said the blonde.

They proceeded to put on a show for him by unbuttoning their shirts so he could see their underwear. They began to flex their legs and the blonde proceeded to show him how flexible she could be. She could put both her feet behind her head. The redhead turned on some music and began to do a sexy dance for him.

"Nice, girls," he said as he felt himself start to become aroused again.

"Blondie, you show me how you can dance now." He liked to direct.

Blondie did as she was told and danced even sexier than the redhead. Then Red leaned back on the arm of the loveseat and spread her legs. She was strong and was able to roll backwards off the love seat into a handstand keeping her legs parted all the while.

"Don't worry," said Red. "We're both on a gymnastics team and do a little dancing on the side, as well. I think we can all have some fun.

He watched as Red started to move closer to Blondie and they both began running their hands over his hot body. He took turns kissing each of them and caressing whatever they offered him. Things were hot and heavy and he needed to sit down.

"Blondie, come over here and have a seat, baby."

Blondie climbed onto his lap and in ten minutes flat, she made him a very happy man. She was small, but very strong. She matched his strength in more ways than one and when they were finished he tossed her aside and grabbed Red.

"So," he said in his sexiest voice, leaning back in the chair. "What are you going to do to make a gorgeous specimen like myself want to be with you?"

"Well, for starters, how's this?" Red pulled him over on to the love seat, and ran her hands all over his back and shoulders. She was giving him the best massage he'd ever had. All over, too! She was good. Real good. When things cooled down, both girls sat on each side of him.

"I think it is your turn to take direction from us," said Red. "You don't get all the fun. Here are the rules. You watch us, but you can't say a single thing. Agreed?"

"You girls are killing me. I'm used to being the boss," he said in an almost whiny voice.

"Agree, or we walk," said Blondie.

Moments in Time...

"Okay, okay. Chill. I'll do it your way," he said. "For now," he added for good measure.

He put his hands behind his head and stretched out to watch whatever show they planned to act out, but really didn't think they could produce any show hotter than what they already had. But they proved him wrong again.

The girls put on different music and began to dance together. Very sensual. Very sexy. Blondie pulled him up to dance with her. It was incredibly erotic the way she moved and moved him. They began making out until he saw what Red was doing. He pulled Blondie down on the couch with him. Red was doing a slow strip tease. She danced as she did so and removed almost everything.

That was all he could take. The three spent the next hour trying to prove who was the master of the game. Just when he thought he had proven no one was as good as he, they would prove him wrong. He was the master, dammit! This had to stop.

"I know you girls think you are so hot that you could melt ice at fifty yards, and it's not that I don't agree. You two are very hot, but no one can compare to the master. I can get any girl, anywhere, at any time and make her mine."

He got up and started fixing his half on, half off clothing. He put his arms around each girl, just to let

Wieland

them know they had just as much a shot with him as any other girl he dated.

"We have a friend that knows you quite well," said Blondie. "She's not all that impressed with you at all. As a matter of fact, she said she'd never date you, not even with a gun to her head."

"That's not possible," he stated getting a little irritated. "There is no one who doesn't want a piece of this." He turned around, showing them his finer points.

Just then, Blondie's aunt stuck her head through the door.

"Don't worry. I'm not looking to join you, although, I wouldn't mind a shot at you, doll." She looked right at him.

"I brought you some drinks. I'm sure you're all pretty thirsty by now. Girls, still looking good." She sat the drinks down and left. They laughed and Red passed out the drinks slipping a 'roofie' into his drink. He never saw it.

They eventually dressed and left the bar heading for the girl's apartment. The walk was short and he was feeling a little dizzy. He figured he must need water. He felt pretty dry. When they reached their destination,

Moments in Time...

they all crashed onto the king -sized bed. Right before he dozed off, his phone rang.

"Hey, big brother. Did you have a good time with my friends tonight?"

He was barely able to talk. Everything was getting blurry and he was seeing double.

"If you set this up, I'll never be able to repay you." His speech was slurred. He noticed Blondie filming him with her phone, but couldn't focus. He gave a little wave just to be friendly. He could see Red in the background, but he wasn't sure that there might be more people there as well. His head was spinning.

"Don't worry about repaying me. It's all been taken care of. Enjoy the last of my friends later tonight." She hung up.

He drifted in and out of sleep with visions of having sex with one, maybe two people? He was even in some pain at one point, but couldn't wake up. All he could remember was bad breath, black hair...out cold.

The next morning, he woke up to sunshine in his face. He remembered most of the evening, but the chick in the night was not ringing a big bell. The television was on with a video of himself having sex with someone. He sat up. Man, he was sore. What the heck? He had to look hard at the TV as his eyesight was still blurry. No sign of the girls.

"Hey lover."

He looked to the other side of the room. There was the manager of the bar, Blondie's aunt. He had just had sex with the ugliest, hairiest, smelliest, female he could possibly imagine.

"What's wrong, lover? Yeah. That's me and you having all kinds of fun."

He leaned over the bed and threw up so hard he thought his insides would come flying out. He vowed to himself to never go bar hopping again. He was done. He'd like to cut a part of his anatomy off right about now. He could kill his sister!

He was finally able to hold his head up and looked over to where she was standing. She was holding his wallet and singing the end of his song.

"Would you walk away from a fool and his money?"

Moments in Time...

Finding Rich

"Now, this is the really interesting part of the whole theater". Nick Wallace was leading some of his family and friends through a tour of the old Chicago Opera House. He and his brother -in -law, Matt Dennison, would be performing with the symphony orchestra in a few days under the direction of his old friend, Dr. Richard Dana.

"I thought Rich would have been here by now," said Nick looking at the time on his cell phone. "He said he would meet us back stage and that was nearly an hour ago."

"It's kind of spooky back here," said Jill Dennison-Wallace, Nick's new wife. She was walking with her hand nearly squeezing the life out of Nick's arm. Each word that was spoken echoed in the vast emptiness of the oldest part of the building.

Wieland

"Yeah, man, I agrees wit' Jill," said Ben Carver, Gerard Wallace's bodyguard. He was a very tall, muscular African American man, but was cowering like a mouse in the darkness. "Anybody gots a flashlight?" Ben was swatting at some cobwebs around his head.

"Oh for the love of God, Ben, quit your bellyaching." Gerard was holding the hand of his girlfriend, Brenda Montgomery. "Just because people say it's haunted, doesn't mean it is. So, quit your whining."

"Help!"

"What was that?" Matt Dennison asked as he stopped walking to look around.

"What was what?" Brenda was grasping Gerard's hand and he was allowing it, which was rare.

Nick used his cell phone to light the area and located a light switch. When he turned it on, they were standing in a large open area with a few ladders against a wall. There was one very tall ladder and Ben was standing right under it."

Ben looked up and knocked the ladder over in his haste to get away. The ladder hit the floor with a resounding noise that was like the sound of a ten- gauge shot gun.

"What the ..." Gerard let go of Brenda and walked over to Ben. "What's the matter with you, man?"

"It be bad luck to walk under a ladder...I done done it now!" Ben started to pace.

Moments in Time...

"Help!"

"There it is again," said Matt. "Can't anyone else hear it?"

"Oh Lawd, Lawd...I hears it too. It gotta be ghosts. I done broughts bad luck down on us all." Ben was pacing and wringing his hands.

"Ben, Ben, calm down," said Jill. "There is no such thing as a ghost."

"Anika, did you..." Matt looked around but there was no sign of Anika Wallace. "Hey, did any of you see where Anika went?" Matt was frantically looking around the backstage area.

"Oh, for Pete's sake!" Gerard held his hands up toward the ceiling. "Everybody just stop. Don't move."

Everyone stopped in their place and slowly looked around. The ceiling was very high with outdated stage lighting equipment, ropes hanging everywhere, buckets, ladders, and dust. Dust everywhere. On everything, along with plenty of cobwebs. Anika was nowhere to be seen.

"Matt, when did you see her last?" Nick had a worried look on his face.

"Oh...Lawd!" Ben was still pacing with his arms raised to the heavens. "What I done did...Lawd!!!"

"Ben," said Jill in a placating tone. "This is not your fault. This is where we agreed to meet Rich. You did not influence us to come back here." She turned to Matt. "And, little brother, I saw you with Anika draped around you just less than fifteen minutes ago over in one of the corners, so you were the last to see her. What was the last thing she said to you?"

Matt had the good grace to look embarrassed. "She said she was going to look for the bathroom."

"And you let her go?" Nick was very upset now.

"Moron," said Gerard. "I can't believe you are really a card -carrying genius!"

Brenda jumped in. "I can't believe Anika is a genius either right now. Who in their right mind goes off in the semi-darkness to look for a bathroom in an old Opera House?"

"Help!"

"Help"

"Lawd...it be dem ghosts," said Ben "Dey done took Miss Anika...Lawd help us!" Ben dropped to his knees with his head in his hands.

"No, wait," said Jill. "There were two cries for help this time. Two different voices. They're way too faint to tell which direction they're coming from."

The group stood still and Ben finally stopped his whimpering. Silence, then...

"Help!" This time there was banging and knocking along with more cries of "help".

Moments in Time...

Nick yelled back. "Keep yelling. We can't tell where you are!"

"We're under the abandoned stage. There's a trap door in the floor. Be careful!"

"Keep making noise," yelled Nick. "We'll find you."

Brenda grabbed Gerard's hand. "Maybe it's Dr. Dana and Anika."

"No way," said Nick. "Rich is the ultimate genius. He teaches the geniuses. There is no way he would get himself into this kind of predicament."

They continued forward slowly looking down at the floor as they went. Gerard grabbed Brenda and pulled her into a darker area of the backstage. He pulled out a silver flask and took a swig and handed it to Brenda.

"I don't know about you, but I'm about sick of all the 'so called' geniuses around here."

Gerard took the flask back from Brenda and took another drink. Then he pulled her to him and started kissing her neck running his tongue softly up to her earlobe. She reached up and pulled him down to her, leaning against him so that she could feel his heartbeat as close as her own. She pulled his mouth to hers and began deep kissing him, pressing him into the wall. Suddenly, she pulled back, took a swig of Gerard's liquor, and hooked her fingers in the waistband of his jeans. She looked him in the eye and smiled. He smiled back, rolling his eyes. He knew what was coming next.

Matt was searching on his hands and knees for the trap door, as was Ben.

"Here it is!" Matt yelled out to the others. The open trap door was off to the side near the moth-eaten curtain edge. "Wow! That is deep!"

"Now we done up and los' Gerard an' Brenda. What we gon' do now? They ain't no steps." Ben was lying flat on the stage trying to see how deep under the stage the opening was.

"We're here to help," yelled Nick into the opening.

"There is a door in here but I can't get it open," said the voice. "I'm not alone down here. A young woman came in the door and tripped on the steps leading down. I think she may be hurt."

"How do we get to the door?" Nick was looking around for Gerard and Brenda while asking.

"Walk back about thirty feet and turn right. I think the door is off a small alcove in that area.

Nick, Jill, Matt, and Ben all turned toward that direction and slowly made their way back to where they had last seen Gerard and Brenda.

"That has to be Anika, down there," said Matt. She must have found the door into the underside of the stage."

Moments in Time...

"Gerard!" Ben was blocking the alcove area with his big body. "Get yo' pants zipped 'fo all these nice peoples see what I'm seein'." He made to pull Gerard out of the area and noticed Brenda trying to hide behind the edge of a curtain.

"Lawd, lawd, lawd," was all Ben could say.

Gerard and Brenda smelled of alcohol. Jill gave them both a dirty look and said to Brenda, "we will be having a conversation about this, as soon as everyone is safe."

"Here's the door!" Matt jerked it open and Anika came tumbling out followed by Dr. Dana.

"Teaches the geniuses, this one," said Gerard sarcastically.

"Great to see you, too, Gerard, and why don't you zip your pants and your mouth," said Dr. Dana. "I see you haven't changed any." He turned to Nick ignoring Gerard's look of shock at being put in his place.

Anika was limping on one foot and Rich was wiping his head with a handkerchief. Anika limped over to Matt. Rich came over to speak privately with Nick. Rich leaned in so only Nick could hear.

"Do you see that fox? I had no idea I was in the closet with such a babe! Jail bait, that one." Rich was eyeing Anika again. "Wow! If only I was twenty years younger!" He stopped long enough to notice the look on Nick's face.

"What?" Rich was confused.

"Rich, I love you, man, but you go anywhere near her and I will have to kill you." Nick had a stern manner about him. "Simple as that. That is my daughter, Anika. Your goddaughter."

"Holy shit!" Rich was astounded at how much Anika had grown up. "She was twelve when I saw her last. Pictures, Nick. Ever heard of those?"

"Hey guys!" Brenda was calling from inside the large closet. "Look at this!"

The others came into the closet and saw that Brenda had located a light switch. Ben barely fit into the room.

"Wow," said Jill. "Look at all these old instruments! They must have been here for a long time."

Looking around the room they could see, a harp, a dulcimer, an old trombone, a bass clarinet, a violin, a saxophone, a trumpet, a guitar and violin and a...

"Oh, my God!" Brenda got on her knees and ran her hands over a strange looking instrument. "Do you know what this is? It's a Hurdy Gurdy!"

"Yes! Yes, it is!" Rich came over to Brenda. "My grandfather used to play one of these! I haven't seen one since I was about ten years old" Rich fondly ran his hand over the instrument, just as Brenda was doing. "These must have been here more than fifty years! But they look in good condition, maybe we can salvage them."

Moments in Time...

Matt was on the floor with Rich and Brenda. He was picking up the different instruments and dusting them off. "This is quite a find," he said. "I wonder if the theater would sell them to us? I would love to have that violin." Anika had joined him.

"Hell, I'll buy the whole lot if we can get out of here before bats start flying up our asses," said Gerard already heading toward the door.

"Come on," said Nick. "We need to go and find out who these really belong to. Then we can decide what we can do with them."

The following morning Nick had managed to arrange for a transport truck to drive all of the instruments to New York City to the Symphony Theater. He and Rich had negotiated a deal to purchase the entire contents of the closet.

"I am excited to have such a rare collection of old instruments," said Rich. "I like your idea, Matt, to repair and fix them up for a short concert as a lead in to our Fall Concert Series."

"I think between the three of us, we can write some original music for this unusual group of instruments," said Nick who was very excited about the whole thing.

"Most of the family is musical and maybe we could use them to play these instruments," said Anika.

"Here we go," said Gerard, rolling his eyes.

Rich took out a notepad and started to plan with Brenda looking over his notes. "Nick has got the dulcimer, Jill you've got the guitar, Anika you can do the violin, hmmm…" Rich looked around. "You'll have to help me, Nick, with the rest."

"Okay, do we know anyone who plays the harp?"

Brenda thought for a minute. "Mamie Gray, the new high school principal, plays. I don't know how good she is, but I bet she would give it a shot."

"Harp, Mamie," said Rich as he wrote. "Saxophone. Anyone?"

When no one answered, Ben spoke up. "I plays the saxophone." He was looking at the ground.

"Ben, saxophone," Rich continued to write with Brenda correcting his spelling.

"Ain't that just grand," said Gerard sarcastically. "Maybe I'll just jump right in and play the Hurdy Gurdy!"

Without missing a beat, Rich said, "Gerard, Hurdy Gurdy."

Brenda noticed the edge of Rich's mouth turn up, trying to keep from grinning. She swatted him on the shoulder.

Matt spoke up. "I can play the trombone."

"Of course, you can," said Gerard. They all ignored him.

Moments in Time...

"That just leaves the bass clarinet and the trumpet," said Rich. "I'll play the trumpet."

Anika came forward. "Doesn't Aunt Shirley play the clarinet? I bet she could play a bass clarinet."

"Aunt Shirley, bass clarinet," said Rich. "Of course, all of this is subject to approval by those listed. That just leaves someone to play the Hurdy Gurdy. That is going to be harder to accomplish, but I have a lot of resources."

Gerard made an artificial coughing sound. "I said I play the Hurdy Gurdy."

"Of course you do, baby," said Brenda.

Everyone looked at him with open mouths. "If you're going to look like that at me, maybe I won't."

The truck was pulling away, heading for New York. The group started to walk down the street with Rich and Nick still discussing this venture.

Gerard was left standing by himself. "Really, guys. I really do play the Hurdy Gurdy." They continued to ignore him. He yelled, "I'm not kidding!"

The group stopped and looked back at him.

"I really do play it." He looked to the side and took a deep breath. "And the bagpipes, too."

The group just looked at Gerard and at each other. Ben broke out in a big laugh.

"Aw'right! We gots us a fam'ly band!"

Gerard joined them as they all continued down the streets of Chicago, planning as they went, the event of the year from a stash of hidden treasures.

Moments in Time...

Friendship & Love Eternal

Silently, he sat on the side of the bed. Watching the clock. Minute by minute. Waiting for the alarm to go off. Sleep had evaded him often the last few nights and he wondered if that might not be a good thing. He jumped as the music of John Lennon came over the clock radio. With resolve, he slowly stood up, ran his hands through his hair, and moved forward into his day.

"Hello!" The Teddy Bear frantically tried to communicate with the man. *"Can't you see me? I am right here where you left me three years ago!"* If he could just move something. Anything! He had been such

an integral part of his owner's life. An unbreakable bond, he couldn't be left behind. Not today, of all days.

"Please, please, don't leave me behind. I came from the best parts of you. I vowed to always be with you. It was what she wanted when she gave me to you. I love you, just like she did."

He came back into the room after his shower with a sadness that spoke of many things he could not change, no matter how hard he tried. He wanted to move faster, but chemo was not something he wanted to beat a path to. He knew many were standing behind him and would continue to support him no matter what this journey might bring. It just wasn't the same as it had been in the past. Sometimes just a touch from another makes all the difference during a time like this.

Something was there, just at the edge of his mind. He couldn't put his finger on it, but it was there none the less. Well, he just didn't have time to think about it for long. If it was that important, it would come to him. He walked to the closet and for some reason he looked up. He smiled. The perfect medicine. Just what he needed!

"Finally, he sees me!" The bear felt himself being taken down from his place on the shelf. *"If I can't do anything else, I can be at his side, like before. That is all I really want. To bring comfort to my human father. My*

Moments in Time...

human mother won't be there but her spirit is with me and it is with him. Does he know it? Yes, I think he does."

He sat in the fairly comfortable recliner, bear by his side, and the attention of some of the best medical people around. There was the usual medical facility noise and jargon all around sounding, at times, like a barnyard. He looked at the workers as he held the bear tight against him. Occasionally someone looked his way. He knew they would be with him soon, so to kill time he began to talk to the bear and the bear answered in his own way.

"Terry, looks familiar, huh?"

"That it does, that it does."

"Just like a bunch of farm animals going about their daily business." He saw one nurse slap her hand down on the counter, throw her head back and laugh loud and deep. "There's the donkey."

"Chickens, lots of those, scurrying from place to place like they can't find a place to roost."

"There's the rooster." He had to keep from laughing out loud when he saw one of the doctor's lean in to one of the prettier, slower moving nurses.

"There's a couple of goats!" Terry watched as two guys from the physical therapy department tried to get

the attention of a new nurse on the floor. *"Horny bunch, they are!"*

He took a deep breath as he picked up the bear and looked it square in the face. "Looks like it's show time." He could see a nurse heading his way. Someone called her name.

"Heeerrrre," she whinnied as she held up her hand to whomever had called her. She looked down at the two of them. "And who do we have here?" She smiled and showed a set of teeth that would make the Osmonds proud.

"Here's the horse."

He couldn't hold it in. He started to laugh and seeing her face, tried to disguise it with a cough.

"Beg pardon," she said. "Did I miss something? Are you okay?"

"Get an apple. Better get an apple, quick!"

He went into another fit of laughter/coughing. "Will you shut up?" He put the bear in the crook of his arm.

"You want me to shut up? I haven't said anything!" The nurse was clearly getting a little touchy.

"Maybe some oats!"

His eyes were watering with the effort to keep from laughing. He took another deep breath and, thankfully, Terry was silent. "I am just a little nervous. I'm sorry."

Moments in Time...

"Totally understandable. I am going to get your IV started and leave you for a bit until your medication comes up from the pharmacy." The nurse was all business now as she skillfully inserted the catheter into his arm. "That should do it for now. Just try to relax." And she trotted away.

"Terry, you nearly got me in trouble!" He picked up the bear and hugged it tight to his chest.

"I love you, too, dad."

He had just shut his eyes when he felt a hand on his shoulder.

Terry was instantly alert as he saw the newcomer standing next to his dad. *"What fresh Hell was this?"*

He looked up. "What…how…when?" He took a breath. He wasn't expecting this.

She set her tote bag next to his chair. "I knew if I said anything, you would not let me come."

"Darn right. You shouldn't be here. Don't…don't sit in that chair! My mother should be in that chair!" Terry was livid. His dad was smiling. *"No…no…just…no."*

"Can I give you a hug?" She didn't wait for an answer, she just leaned in and put her arms around his shoulders. "I'm sorry, that was awkward," she said.

"Wait," he said, and he stood to his feet dropping Terry into the vacated recliner. He reached out and pulled her to him in a big bear hug. "In a million years, I never expected you to turn up here."

She pulled back and put her hand against his cheek. "Friends do for friends. As best they can in any circumstance. I didn't want you to be alone and this was the best I could do in this circumstance. I hope you don't mind too much."

"Hey! Hey! Look down! He is not alone!"

She looked down then, and horror of horrors, she picked him up.

"Terry! I am so glad to meet you! I have heard so much about you!" She hugged him close, just like his dad hugged him. Like she cared.

"Ummm...okay, then. Maybe this isn't the worst thing that could have happened."

They both took their seats and Terry was given the place of honor on his father's lap. The two of them began to talk, jumping from subject to subject, just like on the phone. Every now and then she would reach out and touch Terry like he was included in the conversation, and every now and then she would reach out and lay her hand on his dad's arm or shoulder. The nurse came back with the medication, hung it on the IV pole, and started the infusion into his vein.

"I might fall asleep on you, so if you need to leave..."

Moments in Time...

"Yeah, baby, you can fall asleep on me anytime," said Terry and if he could have winked, he would have done so.

"Terry!" The man said as his eyes started to droop.

"Bears," she said. "What are you gonna do?" She smiled and picked Terry up, kissing him on his teddy bear forehead before placing him next to his dad's heart. Then she kissed the man on the forehead and took his hand in hers. He gave her hand a squeeze as he dozed off knowing that even though everything was not right with his world, it would be one day. Until then, he had the love of Terry and of his good friend. For today, that would do.

"That'll do, pig, that'll do.

Wieland

Moments in Time…

The Reunion

She arrived at the intended meeting place and saw him as soon as she entered the door. It was clear he did not see her. He was very intent on reading the menu. Too intent. She stopped and was not sure what to do next. He was expecting her, but it had been forty- five years since they had seen each other. What to do, what to do! She changed directions and went to sit at the bar.

He was early for their meeting. That's what they had decided to call it, neither wanting to refer to it as a date. He wanted a glimpse of her before she saw him. He was nervous. He could admit it. What would she think of him? They talked every day almost on face book. He knew everything about her. She was very open and told him all of her secrets. He listened and offered advice where he could. He knew she was grateful for his advice and his friendship. She always told him when she failed to follow his counsel. He had looked forward to this meeting all week, but now he felt a little out of his element.

She sat on one of the high stools at the bar in a location that allowed her to see him if she looked sideways. She ordered a glass of Moscoto wine and took a drink. It was so good but she had to be careful. She was not a drinker and any drink containing alcohol had the ability to render her silly or horny. She looked at him. He was still intently looking at the menu. *Must be fascinating,* she thought. She should just go over there. He would think he had been stood up if she waited much longer. Why was she nervous? When they talked on the phone, the conversation never ceased to flow. They talked for hours. She was afraid he would not like how she looked. She was self- conscious about her weight. She wasn't terribly over-weight, but she could stand to lose a few pounds. She was dressed to kill. Very fashionable and funky. *What if he thought she was too old to dress this way?* She wore leggings and long shirts most of the time. She should check her make-up and hair. Okay, enough! She was being ridiculous! She knew him well enough that she knew he didn't care what she looked like. She thought he looked good, though. But she didn't think he would like it if she pointed that out.

He looked up. Hey! She was at the bar. He was sure it was her. Her back was to him, so he could be wrong, but didn't really think so. She must not have seen him. Or didn't recognize him. Or had seen him and changed her mind. What to do! He would like to sneak up on her.

Moments in Time...

Okay, he knew what to do, but damn, she looked better in person than she did in her pictures. He took a drink of his coffee and picked up his phone.

Him: Where are you? Did you stand me up?

Her: No. Just a little nervous. I am at the bar. I can't wait to see you.

Him: Turn around.

She did as he asked and he was within six inches of her. She jumped and spilled wine in her lap. She quickly brushed it off, jumped down off the stool, and threw her arms around him.

"Oh, my God," she squealed nearly deafening him. "It's you! Really you!" He had put his arms around her in a hug as well. She backed off a little leaving her hands on his shoulders. She looked him in the eyes and slowly lowered her mouth to his, kissing him softly on the corner of his lips. She smiled and so did he.

"Coffee, yuck," was all she said.

He gave her another hug and took her hand leading her to the table. "I got a cup for you, too," he said. "Black. I think you'll like it." He burst out laughing at the look on her face.

"Okay, dude. That was uncalled for." She squeezed his hand before she let it go and sat at the table. He had ordered her iced tea. He had remembered she had said she liked tea. So far, she was very impressed.

Wieland

He sat opposite her and said he had not seen her come in. She confessed she had seen him but felt very self- conscious and retreated to the bar. The waiter came to the table to see if they knew what they wanted to order.

"I'm sure *he* does," she said in a giddy tone. "He was reading that menu for quite a while when I got here."

"No, I was not." He looked around and then leaned forward to speak. "I was hiding behind it, afraid you would spot me." He laughed. "Honestly, I didn't see a thing on it!"

She laughed too at the annoyed look on the waiter's face. "Give us a minute, would you?" The waiter started to leave. "Wait! I would like another glass of Moscoto," she said.

"Very good, and for you, sir, anything else to drink?"

"What do you have on tap?"

She looked at him while he and the waiter discussed what was available on tap. He looked good to her. She felt like she was on a first date in her teenage years. A little shy, a little bold, and not sure what to say. When she was on face book with him, she had time to compose her thoughts. This was spur of the moment. She did spur of the moment well, in fiction. Not so much in real life.

When the waiter left, they both picked up the menu and glanced at it. She spoke first. "I have a hard time making a food decision, from my childhood, you know…"

"I know," he said. "We are both diabetic. How about we make it easy and both have a chicken Caesar salad?" He had a hopeful look on his face.

"I can eat that," she said.

He had not realized he had been holding his breath until the waiter left. He watched the waiter leave and then looked at her. "You look good."

"Thank you. You do as well. I can't tell you how good it is to see you," she said. She took his hands in hers across the table and he allowed it. He even gave her hands another squeeze.

"I never thought I would ever get to see you again." She was thinking about all of the times she had asked if she could see him and he had declined.

"I wasn't so sure myself for a while." He looked down and she knew he was thinking about his deceased wife.

She stood up and came around to sit in the chair on the same side of the table as he was sitting. She reached out and hugged him tight against her. She took her hand and ran it through the hair on the back of his head. It was meant to be a comforting gesture.

 It was anything but, to him. When she pulled away, he felt like something was missing. Warmth, maybe?

Their food came and she moved back to her side of the table and they began to eat. Something had changed and they began to talk like the old friends they were. They laughed, teased, cried a little, and made up for forty- five years apart. After the meal was over, he stood up and reached for her hand.

"It is warm out tonight and the moon is full. Want to take a walk?"

"I would love it," she said and stood up taking his hand.

They walked along the shore of the river, slowly, still in conversation about any and everything. They realized at the same time that they were still holding hands. They looked at each other.

'It's okay for friends to hold hands, right?" She started to pull her hand away and he stopped her.

He took hold of her other hand and pulled her to him.

Not good, she thought. She'd had three glasses of wine and was having a hard time thinking straight as it was.

"I have had too much wine and I need to apologize for my behavior in advance. You know I am not after you," she said.

"I know that," he replied. "We have discussed it often. Plus, you know I can get any girl I want. No problem." He was trying to lighten the mood because he had feelings rising like the tides and that was very unexpected.

"Then forgive me when I do this." She pulled in tighter and put her lips to his. He was still for a minute, but just a minute. She began to move her lips against his, small sexy kisses that she doubted he was prepared for.

He began to respond. He was meeting her kisses and returning as much as he knew how. He had been out of practice, but he had to say, she was an excellent kisser. *Well, two can play this game*, he thought. He opened his mouth wider and deepened the kiss. He could tell she had not expected that and he was glad he had gotten one over on her.

"Wow," he said against her lips.

"Do you have any idea what I want to do with you right now?" She kept her lips against his and they spoke very softly as if they could not bear to lose the contact.

"Umm... I think I have some idea." He deepened the kiss once again. "I remember how you wrote us kissing in your short story."

"Do you now," she said. She responded by sucking his lower lip before she sucked his tongue into her mouth. "We were very advanced for our ages." She continued the deep kissing and running her hands through his hair. She slowed to a stop and pulled back a little, but he still wanted the contact and leaned forward, keeping his lips close to hers. She began to kiss and run her tongue over his neck.

"Have you figured out what I want yet?" She continued to explore his neck while she spoke.

"Yes, I am quite sure I know what you want. We want the same thing. I am not sure it is wise, but, God help me, I want it too."

"Then we should go to your house and do it," she said. "Right now, before the mood leaves."

"I don't think the mood will leave," he responded. "And if it does, one of your kisses will bring it back."

"Maybe we should just go to my motel. It is closer," she said in a voice that was very sexy to him. "Baby, I know they have one in the back lobby by the auditorium."

He stopped cold and pulled back. "One what? Are we on the same page?"

"A piano, of course, what did you think I meant? I have wanted to hear you play since we reconnected. You know that," she said with a laugh. "What did you think I meant?"

"Well...the piano, of course," he laughed to hide his embarrassment of getting the wrong signals from her.

"Let's go. I'll follow you." Probably better that they not go to his house. She had told him, she hoped she would be able to drive back to the motel after dark. That way when they finished with the piano, she could go straight to her room for the night and he could go home.

Her motel was pretty deserted this time of night in this area. The store close by was closed for the night. A few people were in the bar, but there was music and it was doubtful anyone in there would hear him at the piano. It was situated outside the auditorium, near the back door to the place.

"Do you mind to play for me?" She had a hopeful look on her face.

He was still reeling from all the unexpected kissing and he found himself floundering between being embarrassed that he had let it happen and wanting it to continue. His thought was that it must not have affected her the same way as it had him. This had been a very big step for him. He knew it was not quite as big a step for her.

"Sure. I will play. Will you sing with me?"

"Maybe, if you play something I know," she said a little nervously. "My voice needs a lot of warm up to sound good and you know my forte is show tunes and opera. I will probably sound like crap, but I will try if you don't laugh." She sat on the bench next to him.

A little too close, considering what had taken place earlier. He began to play some old pop songs and after a bit, to sing a little with them.

She flagged the bartender when he passed and asked for a couple of glasses of wine. He knew her and brought them a bottle of Moscoto on the house. He gave her a wink and returned to the bar.

"Do you know him?" He had stopped playing.

"I have stayed here often and he knows the wine I like. He also knows I was hoping to hear my friend play the piano," she said. She poured the wine and they both took a drink. Then she took a few more drinks and emptied her glass.

"Kick it up a notch, baby, for me," she said looking a little sleepy. She put her head on his shoulder and her arm around his waist.

He began to play everything he could think of and noticed the more he played the more she looked uncomfortable. He remembered something she had said to him a long time ago about how pianists turned her on. Better be careful or this could go where no man should at this time.

"I think this will be the last song," he said. "You know it. We can sing it together, then I really have to go. This old man is getting a little tired and I still have to drive home." They laughed and had a great time with the song. When it was over, he closed the cover on the piano keys.

They looked at each other.

Moments in Time...

"I have something for you," she said. "But you will have to come to my room to get it."

"Is that wise?" He was feeling very mellow and he could tell she was too. He'd had a great time, but was still confused about all the kissing earlier. At least it did not seem to have affected the friendship.

"Very wise, old friend. You are a kid. I am an old lady. What do you think is going to happen?" She took his hand and led him down the hall to her room.

"Here we are. Come on in," she said. "I have cheese and crackers as well as nuts, and fruit. I had it brought up from room service. I didn't want you to drive home with just wine in your system."

He looked at the tray, then at her, then the room. She had sexy underwear on the bed and sexy nightgowns. He wondered if that had been staged. He was starting to sweat.

"Baby, I know what you are thinking and I did not lay those out for you to choose from." She scooped them all up and threw them in the suit case. "Come here. Sit with me."

He sat on the side of the bed with her and she picked up a piece of melon and fed it to him. Then a piece of pineapple. He stopped her when she picked up the strawberry and took it from her. He took a bite and offered it to her for a bite. She took it.

Wieland

He leaned in for the softest of kisses on her cheek. Then he kissed her softly on the lips. She responded in a more aggressive manner. She heated the kiss up. He responded and ran his hand from her head down her back and pulled her tighter. He deepened the kisses as he had earlier, but this time they kept their eyes open. It was clear to both that they knew what they were doing.

She lay back on the bed and pulled him down on top of her. The kisses changed to hot and passionate. Their hands were no longer quiet as they spoke a different language all their own. They had become very intimate and very hungry.

They pulled a little apart as he was removing his shirt, and hers. "What are we doing?" they said together.

"I am not going to lie," he said. "I want you tonight and not in just a friendly way, if you know what I mean.

"I know very well that you want me. You can't hide that fact and I want you too, but here's the thing. I am not sure either one of us is ready for this. It is too soon for you and probably for me too." She took his face in her hands and kissed him, biting his lip as she did.

"That's not helping," he said with a smile. "I know you are right. You have gone through a lot these past few months as well. This is hard…no pun intended. Let's eat and talk for a bit."

Moments in Time...

They laughed and joked while they ate the food that had been provided. They fed each other and threw it up into the air and tried to catch it. They finally finished and she turned the radio on, put his arms around her and said she wanted one dance before he left.

She put her back to him and pulled his arms tighter around her. He put his head against hers and they just swayed a little to the music. When it was finished, they kissed one last time. She led him to the door.

"When you are ready to take a step like we almost did, you will know. It may not be with me as, like you said, you can get any girl you want." She smiled and so did he. "You are very popular with the ladies and I am not sure I can stand the competition. I have never been anyone's first choice and I know I would not be in this case either."

"Why would you say that?" he was looking puzzled.

"Now you have had a taste of the kind of pleasure you could have once again and that does not go away easily. Believe me, I know." She pulled him to her. "Do you understand?"

"I do understand. I am not sure what you are suggesting, but I think I know what you mean. We are good friends. Sex messes things up and you are right. I am not ready for that at this stage of things."

"We have a lot of love in friendship. I don't want to lose that," she said with tears in her eyes.

"Neither do I," he replied.

"When you are ready, you will know. You will feel it in your gut. In your heart. You are not a one night stand kind of guy, and if you wanted to be, I am not the girl for that. I care way too much for you to go that route. Am I making sense?"

"You are. You sound like your messages," he said. "I had a great time. I'd like to have more. Thank you for a great time tonight."

"When that time comes and you know that you know, if I am around, feel free to contact me and we will see what happens. Agreed?"

"Agreed." He pulled her close and gave her one hell of a devastating kiss. "Don't you forget me either. You are quite popular too."

"We will just continue as usual, like nothing has changed and when the time is right, we will both move forward with or without each other." They both looked a little sad.

He opened the door. She gave another quick kiss and he was gone.

She picked up the left -over debris and got ready for bed. She could still feel his kisses and she was still hot from his piano playing. He had no idea how that had affected her.

He had been gone for at least an hour and she was still lying in bed, awake, thinking about the evening. She

Moments in Time...

wanted him. She could not deny it. But she could not be a one night stand. That, she was sure she had made clear. She was starting to drift off when she heard it. It sounded like a soft knock at the door.

She sat up not hearing anything further. She was starting to get back under the covers when she heard it again, harder this time. She got up and opened the door to find him standing there...

Wieland

Moments in Time...

The Good Old Days

"Just so you all know," said Xia Delacourt, "I don't belong here." She adjusted the oxygen cannula to fit better in her nose and took a few deep breaths. The oxygen was her lifeline, though she hated it. She was restless. There was too much humidity today! She took a drink of water from the small glass provided by the community program to which she belonged.

"Can you sit still? You are driving me nuts. Now, knock it off!" This came from the younger woman to her left, a shorter, bustier woman reminiscent of a less artificial Dolly Parton. Yvette Conners, also on oxygen, but not as dependent as Xia. Yet.

"Both of you need to settle down," said Zada Moovey. "Bingo is getting ready to start and I need to win me some shampoo and some Crisco."

The other two looked at her like she was stark naked in a room full of vipers.

"Crisco!" Yvette almost yelled. "They don't have no Crisco on the bingo cart."

"Keep your voices down," yelled Xia. "What is the matter with you, Zada? Your mind gets worse every day! All you need is for that new nurse to hear you say that. We're about the only sane ones in this place. Look around!"

"All three of you old crones need to shut yer pie holes," said the old man in the electric wheelchair at the other end of the table. "Some of us are tryin' to think straight!"

"You couldn't think straight if I put a gun to your head," yelled Xia as loud as she could. "Now you shut up before I have to come down there and shut you up."

"She has done it before," said Yvette. "I seen it".

"Bring it on, bitches," said the old man. "I, too, have seen way more of you three than even you can remember." He tipped his dusty black hat, turned his wheelchair and left without giving them a chance to respond.

The other little man sitting at the end of the table began to laugh at the three of them. With a look from Xia, he shut up fast and put a bingo chip in his mouth.

"Shut up and eat your bingo chips!" Zada was in no mood for this shit today. "Like I said, things just ain't the same. I miss the old days when we could do anything we wanted and get paid to do it."

Moments in Time...

"Them was some good old days, though," said Yvette. "Xia, pick out our usual cards. Three each." She looked wistful. "I remember when we could handle 'three each' without so much as batting an eye." She laughed at her attempt at a joke. Zada joined in, but Xia just looked at them both and with a shake of her head, began to arrange her cards the way she liked.

Later, after bingo was done and lunch had been served, the three were eating quietly when Yvette suddenly put down her fork and looked at the other two. "Do either of you ever think about the old days when we worked as a team?"

"Think about it? I dream about it," said Zada with her hands folded in a prayer-like fashion. "If only we could go back forty odd years, I would do so many things differently."

"What," said Xia in a sarcastic voice, hands on hips. "Move a tad faster? Spend less time in front of a mirror? Remember where you hid the map?"

"Shut up, Xia! Do you want everyone in the place to hear you?" Yvette shoved her food away. "If Zada hadn't lost that map, we would all be in a different place in our lives. Not dependent on a state agency for help just to live."

"You stole the damn thing," said Xia. "What made you give it to Zada in the first place?"

"Hey!" Zada stood up with her cane. "It always comes back to me, doesn't it? It was a team effort ladies. Not one of us did this on our own!" She stalked off toward the bathrooms as was her custom when conversation got dicey.

"She'll be back," said Yvette. "By the time it takes her to get to the bathroom, use it, and walk back here, she will have forgotten the ill feelings."

"She's right, though." Xia was finger combing her hair trying to get it into an elaborate, Victorian-looking barrette. "It was all of us together. We can't blame her. She overheard that rich man, Bob, talking about his robbing that bank and hiding the money. Bragging about it, actually. He was talking to that skinny, dirty guy, Fred, I think his name was."

Yvette got up to help Xia fix her hair. Taking a comb and as Xia held her head back, Yvette wound her longish white hair in a thin bun and expertly applied the barrette. Yvette had been a hair stylist in her younger years, but had not lost her touch. Occasionally she helped one of the nurse's aides fix some of the other client's hair. That is, if her arthritis in her hands was not too bad. The barrette was a keepsake from their younger, wilder days.

"I remember it like it was yesterday," said Yvette. "Bob was a looker. One of the best I ever had. Big tipper too. Fred, well, I always hated to see him come in. He had a bad smell. Kerosene, I think. Dirty clothes, dirty hair, yellow teeth. I handed him a toothbrush once and he asked me what it was for. He says to me, he says 'Are you a wantin' me to put this up your…'"

"Yvette!" Zada had returned to the table and had heard most of the conversation. "Watch what you say here. How many times do I have to say that? People can hear you!"

"They might hear us, but most can't remember nothin' any longer than a hot fart stays in the air, and the others are deaf." said Xia looking around to see who might have heard.

They saw one of the nurses heading their way and tried to look busy so as not to be singled out.

"Shit, she's coming for us. Damn you Yvette," said Xia. "You attracted her attention by messing with my hair."

"No, look who is with her," said Zada. "That old blow hard is heading back here with the pastor."

"Afternoon, Pastor," said Xia standing up. "Oh, looky there!" She pointed to the doors leading to the outside patio at the end of the room. "They are going to plant flowers today. We can't miss that." She started in that direction with her four-wheeled walker. Zada and Yvette looked at each other and the grinning old man in the electric wheelchair. He was flipping them off behind the pastor's back.

"You can run, but you can't hide," he said.

Xia stopped, turned around, and smiled a fake smile at the old man and the pastor. She blew him a kiss as the pastor turned to leave.

The old man looked at each of the three ladies. "Some things never change" He tipped his hat. "Ladies. Or should I say, Madams." He turned and parked his chair near the scrawny old man still at the end of the table and pulled out a deck of cards.

The three ladies continued on out the open doors and found seats away from the others working around the flower box.

"He called us Madams. That can't be a coincidence," said Zada.

"For piss sakes," said Xia. "What are the odds of one of our former customers recognizing us here?"

"What is that old geezers name anyway?" Yvette went over to the door and looked in. She motioned for one of the nurse's aides. She stood talking with her for a few minutes, then looked over at Xia and Zada. Her face was pale. The aide gave her a hug and Yvette returned to her seat with the other two.

"You aren't going to believe this," she said.

"What won't we believe? I'm on pins and needles," said Xia in a bored voice as she tried to catch her breath.

Moments in Time...

Yvette looked around to see if anyone was in hearing distance and in a hushed voice she replied. "His name is Bob."

"So?" Xia remained bored.

"Oh, my God!" Zada jumped up. "It's Bob finally come for me. He knows I took his map!"

"Don't be ridiculous," said Xia. "Bobs are a dime a dozen."

She sat back down. "I guess you're right. No reason to get alarmed."

"Let's look back for a moment," said Yvette. "Back to that day when we were in our prime. Do you both remember?"

"Madam X," said Xia. "For Madam X rated."

"Madam Y," said Yvette, "for Madam Y not?"

"Madam Z," said Zada. "Ze vun zey all vant."

Those were the good old days to these three old ladies. Each had a look of pride on their face. They had torn up the town in those days. Xia had a booming brothel with more business than she could handle. Besides herself, she had two local 'girls' that worked part time when they could get away from home.

Yvette had a smaller 'cat house' as it was known in a seedier town about five miles from Xia's place. She worked it alone since business was not as good. The town was dying and she could barely pay her bills. She needed more customers. Some days she only had five customers. At five- dollars a pop, that was not much.

Zada, on the other hand had a very successful business about ten miles away in an industrial town. She could not keep up with business. Men came every day after work from the local plant just to see her. She played a character that was supposed to be from France. It was a turn on for most of the men. Unfortunately, the plant closed down and she found her clientele was not as loyal as she would have thought. After all, she was indeed 'Madam Z." Zey all vanted her. She repeated that as her mantra.

Each lady had heard of the other two. Needing help, Xia offered to each of the others a chance to work for her at her large operation. Both accepted. They became widely known as Madams X, Y, and Z or the 'Alphabet Brothel' as it was whispered about.

Then 'Bob' showed up. They had been working together for about three years when he first made an appearance. Tall, dark, handsome as hell, with a sweet-talking tongue that could talk a nun out of her virtue. He took turns with the ladies. He kept even among them, never expressing whether or not he had a favorite. They all liked him, or so they said.

Zada had been sipping tea in the living room and tallying up the days 'business'. Bob was a customer that evening and was with Yvette. A small, unkempt man that he had brought along, was with Xia. Zada was dreading when they left because she knew that Xia would be hateful and sarcastic the rest of the night because she hated the smelly customers that, on occasion, came her way. She usually fielded them to the other two. However, Bob was insistent that Fred be with Xia, and he was willing to pay three times the going rate for it. Xia had been a former gymnast and track star in her younger days, and Fred had a thing for that according to Bob. Fred really never said much.

As Zada counted, she began to hear doors closing and a conversation going on between Bob and Fred. She was not supposed to eavesdrop on the clients but she had a healthy curiosity, or nosiness, as Xia called it.

"You pulled a gun on them?" Fred had excitement in his voice. Zada froze to hear who a gun had been pulled on.

"Right in the bank! You pulled out a gun!" Fred said this as a statement and not a question. "How did you get away?" Fred was talking with much hero worship in his voice.

"I fired two shots into the ceiling and everyone hit the deck." Bob was washing is hands in the hallway bathroom. "Then they just started piling the cash into the suit case I had. No body made a move after that."

Zada could hear him trying to get a paper towel out of the dispenser. She knew that would take him a few minutes. They really needed to fix that. She had to remember to mention it again to Xia. *Damn! Here they come! I better hide!* She jumped over the back of the couch just before the two men sat down on it. *Shit! That was close!*

She tried not to breathe but she had the heel of her shoe caught in the hem of her dress. She was almost in a fetal position and it was very uncomfortable.

"I left that place with over five hundred thousand dollars in that suitcase. Best heist I ever pulled," bragged Bob.

"Hot damn! What did you do with the money?" Fred was on the edge of his seat engrossed in the outcome.

"I hid it where no one will ever find it. I am set for life." Bob pulled out a piece of paper from the inside of his jacket pocket. "I drew this map to the hiding place, you know, in case I was to forget where I hid it."

"What are you two still doing here?" Xia had returned from cleaning up with Yvette right behind her.

"Did you pay Zada yet?" Yvette was looking around.

"We ain't seen Zada, so we was waiting for you gals. We're ready to pay and get out of this dump," said Fred.

"Where'd she go?" Xia walked over to the screen door and looked out into the yard. "Zada!" She yelled out the door. When she got no response, she looked into the hallway. "Zada! Where could she have gone?"

Moments in Time...

She turned to go back into the living room where both men were feigning interest in finding Zada while really hoping to get out of there without paying for services rendered. She saw the top of a red head peek over the back of the couch at the same time that Yvette did. Zada had her finger over her mouth imploring them to keep quiet and not give her away.

Xia and Yvette had shocked looks on their faces. The men noticed.

"What's the matter? You gals gone daft?" Bob was getting up. Zada dropped down behind the couch again.

"Yeah, maybe," said Yvette realizing something was wrong.

"Why don't you folks have this one for free," said Xia. "You know, since this is Fred's first time here and we'll see you boys in a couple of days."

"Well! Okay then!" Bob and Fred headed out the door, tipping their hats as they went.

Xia slammed the door. "Get your skinny ass out from behind that couch, Zada! I almost pissed in my panties, if I had been wearing panties, when you popped up behind there."

"Somebody help me out. My heel is caught, dammit!"

Yvette had gone over to help Zada out and Zada proceeded to tell them what she had heard.

"Good Lord!" Xia sat with her head in her hand leaning on the table. "If we could find that money, we would never have to work again in our lives."

"Think, ladies," said Yvette. "There must be some way."

They talked well into the wee hours of the morning that night. Finally, they had a fool proof plan to get the map from Bob and two days later, when the guys returned, they put the plan into action.

They plied the men with wine while Xia turned up the music and performed a rousing Tango with Bob, including a rose between her teeth. Zada had drawn the short straw and had taken Fred to her room while Yvette manned the cash box.

Eventually, Xia led a slightly tipsy Bob into her room and stripped him of his clothing placing it near the door. She had then tied him to a post, facing away from the door, got her riding crop and had donned her leather outfit for those that liked a bit of pain. She snaked the crop over Bob's skin as he laughed and cried out at the same time. After Xia was satisfied that she had done all she could do with Bob in this position, she tied Bob's hands above him to her gymnast bar that crossed the room overhead. *Where in the hell was Yvette?* She had to continue. She jumped up to grab the bar, swung her legs over it and hung upside down with her face in Bob's, shall we say, happy place.

Moments in Time...

She had started her business when she finally heard the door open a crack and Yvette's head look in. Xia, still hanging upside down, pointed to the jacket and waved her away. She stared a minute or two, made a face, grabbed the jacket and shut the door. After a few minutes, the door opened again and a hand replaced the jacket.

"Okay, time is up, thank God, and you need to dress, pay Yvette, and leave," said Xia wiping her mouth. "In other words, get the hell out."

She had untied Bob. "Okay I'm going, sweet thing. That was the best yet," said Bob slurring his words. He dressed while Xia watched to make sure he didn't notice the map had been exchanged for a phony one.

After the men had gone, they gathered in the living room to look at the map. It was a little hard to follow but Xia figured it out. Tomorrow, they would look for the suitcase of money and live the rest of their lives in luxury. They finished two bottles of wine and when they went to bed, Zada had been given the map for safe keeping.

The next morning, Zada could not find the map. Yvette remembered her saying that she would put it in a place no one could find in case Bob ever realized he had the phony map and came looking for it. They looked for weeks, but were never able to recover the map. Bob also never returned. She heard he was busted for having two wives and was sent to jail for a few months.

In another few months, the city cracked down on prostitution and Xia's business was shut down. They escaped jail time by agreeing to leave the town and never return.

They had reunited nearly fifty years later when they found themselves part of this state run program. Each had qualified for assistance and they found themselves at the community room three days each week. Now they were faced with the possibility that Bob had come after them. The map was gone forever.

"In you go, ladies," said the aide. "It is about to rain." They had failed to notice the storm clouds gathering while they were reminiscing about the past and what they might do if Bob was indeed, Bob, and came after them.

"Look how bad Xia is," Zada said to Yvette. "She can't walk from here to there without nearly collapsing from shortness of breath."

"I think she isn't long for this world," said Yvette. They made it to the table and waited nearly ten minutes for Xia to make it all the way across the room.

When she finally arrived, she looked at them both and shook her head. "Remind me not to ask for help from either one of you. I could die waiting for that." She had nearly collapsed trying to get the words out. The nurse rushed over to check her pulse oximetry and listen to her lungs.

Moments in Time...

"Same as always," she said. "You look like you are ready to keel over and your pulse ox is better than mine."

The three sat there waiting for their bus to be called to take them home. Bob pulled up in his electric wheelchair.

"Bitches," he said tipping his hat. "Madam X, Madam Y, Madam Z. Figure it out yet?"

"Figure what out, asshole?" Xia tried to stand. "We don't have your damn map!"

"I know that," stated Bob in a matter of fact manner. The three ladies looked at each other.

"There never was a map. There never was a suitcase. I made the whole thing up," said Bob. "I knew Zada would have her nose in whatever Fred and I were discussing."

"Is that right?" Xia put a hand on her hip.

"Sure it is," said Bob. "I think I would know if I had robbed a bank."

"You don't know your own name on a good day, you old fart," said Xia. "Well, ladies, I guess we were worried for nothing."

"Son of a bitch!" Zada was about to blow a gasket. " You sorry sack of shit! For nearly fifty years, I have wondered what I did with the map that could have put us all on easy street and you tell us now that the whole thing was a joke?" She took her cane and whacked it over Bob's head.

"Ouch!" Bob tried to cover his head while Fred just sat there and laughed. He put his chair in gear and started away from the table. Zada right behind him. A few feet away, Bob rounded on them in his chair and pulled out a gun, pointing it straight at Zada's heart.

"Oh no you don't!" Xia whipped her oxygen off, jumped up on the table, did a summersault in the air and landed at Bob's feet. She grabbed the gun from him and smacked him over the head with it while everyone in the room sat in stunned silence.

She realized what she had done. "I've been healed! It's a miracle!" She couldn't pull it off. The new nurse had seen the whole thing. She walked over to Xia.

"You had better tell us what is going on. I am quite sure you no longer qualify for the program."

Xia looked at Zada's and Yvette's stunned faces. "I'm sorry," she said before addressing the whole room. "I might be old, but I just won a senior's marathon in Idaho two months ago. And I jog every day. Oh, and I am a black belt in Karate." She put her hands on her walker and did a handstand. After dismounting, she addressed the transportation staff.

"I still need a ride home."

Everyone returned to their seats and Bob was taken to a room and the door shut to await the police. The

Moments in Time...

doctors were called in and most of the whole place was consumed with that. Finally the three ladies were alone. The nurse wandered over and sat at the table with them, where Zada and Yvette were still in shock. They had all been given some Gatorade to drink.

"Are you okay Grandma?" She looked at Xia. "I brought the suitcase like you asked. It was just where you said it would be in your attic."

Yvette and Zada's mouths dropped open. "I thought Bob said the map was a phony," said Yvette.

"Yeah, I don't understand," said Zada.

"Okay, look," said Xia. "The map was real. Bob did rob a bank. I did occupy him while Yvette took the map from his jacket pocket. Sorry, honey." She said to her granddaughter.

"Then you must have found the map after I lost it," said Zada with disbelief on her face.

"No, no," replied Xia with little remorse. "You remember we drank all that wine after we got the map." They all agreed that they had.

"Zada, you gave the map to me to hold on to. You didn't think you were responsible enough to be the one to keep it. After all, you were the youngest." Xia put a hand on her shoulder when Zada started to cry from sheer relief.

"I didn't lose it." She put her head in her hands.

Wieland

Xia called them closer. "After we were busted, I followed the map and collected the suitcase. Almost all of the money is still there, I invested some of it to live on and now the three of us will never want for anything the rest of our lives. I will get the two of you the best possible healthcare and we will all live happily ever after."

The nurse, an author, sat back looking at the three of them. Two with oxygen and one struggling to walk straight with her cane. "Well, what do you think?" She put the papers she had been reading back into her story folder. "Do you want me to publish it or not?"

"I don't know," said Joan. "I think the ending is weak. I should have had two men waiting on me hand and foot. I don't go for that happy ever after shit. I don't think I like it. You need to re-write that story."

"I don't like my name. I told you to use a different name. The one I sent you," said Deb.

"I don't look like Dolly Parton. Can my boyfriend be in it?" Stella was passing out the bingo cards to their table and Joan was looking through them for their favorite cards.

"There is no way I can make all three of you happy with this story. I can re-write the end if you like. I can make you end up married to Bob, Joan."

"Hell, no," said Joan. "Just leave it like it is. Go on and do your nurse stuff. It's time for bingo."

Moments in Time...

"Okay, see you in the neb room at eleven."

And the day continued as every day does in the lives of the elderly in the state run program. But once in a while, if you work it right, you can make a difference in the lives of some very special older folks.

This story is dedicated to Joan Larock, Stella Townley, and Deb Berry, three ladies I have had the privilege of working with for the past four years. It has been a pleasure.

Acknowledgements

I would like to take a few minutes to acknowledge those who made this book possible. First and foremost, I would like to thank Richard Diakun, my friend of more than forty-five years, for the inspiration for this book. I have not seen him in as many years but reconnected on social media with the release of my first book. We were each other's first love and by asking me a simple question from our teenage years, did I remember the song that was playing when we shared our first kiss, a question I was unable to answer, the idea for this book was born. Richard has been my main reader throughout all of my writing and has suggested or challenged me to write almost all of the stories in this book. He also plays a part in many of the stories that are written here. Thank you, Richard, so much for your help, suggestions, beautiful music selections, and all the time you put into reading and critiquing my work.

Also, many thanks to Paula Hawkins, my first beta reader. She has been with me from the beginning with encouragement and friendship. You have made a real difference in how my book signings have gone. You are just too much fun! Thank you to a special beta reader, Gladys Barrington, for reading everything I have written and giving me good feedback to it all. Much thanks go out to all of the more recent beta readers. Gini Hawkins, Trichia West-Ellerby, and Evelyn Crow Smith. You guys are the best.

About the Author

The only constant in this world is change and in my life, there has been more than enough with more looming on the horizon. I am currently working on more than one book at a time and enjoying writing short stories more than I can tell you.

I am currently still living in Michigan, but I am sad to say my mother passed away in January 2017, peacefully, may I add. I feel like a part of me left with her but at the same time part of her lives on within me. I miss her with every breath. She lived to be ninety-six years old.

As I am writing this, I am thinking about all the author friends I have met over the past year. I have also reconnected with some old friends in my hometown of Williamsburg, Virginia, and am considering this town as a possible place to relocate. Although I am sure I will miss my boys, Scott and Steven, as well as my grandson, Liam, I am continuing to live life to the fullest as much as possible. And I wish the same for all of my readers!

Made in the USA
Columbia, SC
03 July 2017